Lords
of Air and
Darkness

Also by Quentin Dodd

Beatnik Rutabagas from Beyond the Stars

The Princess of Neptune

Tennis Camp of the Living Dead

Tommy Frasier and the Planet of the Slugs

Tommy Frasier and the Asteroid Bats

QUENTIN DODD

Snake Year Press

Snake Year Press
Crawfordsville, Indiana
www.snakeyearpress.com

www.quentindodd.com/darkness

ISBN-13: 978-1-7337291-0-9
LCCN: 2019902015

For V.Z., Wilson, and Wes

This book is a work of fiction.

1

It was early in June when all this started. School had been out for a couple of weeks, and I had been working at my aunt Jaya's restaurant ever since. I was sweeping the floor and checking the napkin dispensers when she called, "Hal! Delivery!" and held up a paper bag with an order ticket stapled to the top.

"Okay." I stowed my broom and picked up the bag. It was full of good-smelling white cartons wrapped in foil. I hadn't been working there long enough to be sick of the smell of Korean food, and I wondered if that was going to happen by the end of the summer. I hoped not. In my family, eating at Jaya's restaurant had always been sort of a treat, involving a special trip all the way downtown and a selection of food we never saw otherwise. So far, even when I was bussing tables or cleaning the bathroom, I still felt like I was part of something unusual and interesting. I hoped that would last.

Everyone called the restaurant "Jaya's," but its full name was "Jaya's Authentic Foods." My aunt had opened it up years and years ago, right after she married my uncle Tim and moved to America. Back then, her English still had training wheels, which is why the name sounds more like a grocery store than a restaurant, but after being in business for so long, she doesn't see any reason to change it.

I checked the order ticket as I headed through the kitchen toward the back door. 1151 River Park Drive. That was all the way on the other side of town. I grabbed one of the insulated carriers from the peg by the door and zipped it around the paper bag. Even then, I was going to be pushing it to get all the way out there before the food started to go lukewarm. I hurried into the alley and got into my worn-out old Honda Civic. When I put the carrier on the passenger seat, I checked the order sheet one more time. That was when I noticed the name Jaya had written above the order.

John Graze.

Whoa. For real?

John Graze is our local celebrity. Well, he is to me. If you know all of Ronnie James Dio's guitar players, or if you can name at least one Mercyful Fate album, maybe he's a celebrity to you, too. His band, Left Hand Ritual, used to scare the hell out of people back in the 1980s. Even now, when the portraits on the backs of their albums look goofy and quaint, their music is still some pretty creepy stuff. They were sort of a cross between Candlemass and W.A.S.P., but if you aren't a big enough

8

fan of 1980s metal to know what that means, then just trust me. They're awesome

I love that kind of music. I love the way it sounds when I throw a garage-sale metal tape into my car's temperamental old cassette deck. I love looking at the unbelievable art on the album covers, and I love the way the bands looked back then. It was all so theatrical. With their gigantic hair and steel-reinforced costumes, they all looked like space pirate opera singers from another dimension.

After he split with Left Hand Ritual, John Graze disappeared for few years, but he eventually ended up back in his old home town of Lamasco, Indiana. When I put it that way, it sounds like he stumbled off a Greyhound and collapsed onto a park bench, but in reality, he bought a mansion. People with mansions get a lot of things delivered to them, which was where I came in.

I backed out of the alley, drove north for a couple of blocks, then got onto the expressway and headed east. Soon I was out of the center of the city, past the office buildings, the factories, and the row-house neighborhoods. I drove as fast as I could without making myself conspicuous. Technically, 1151 River Park Drive wasn't in Lamasco at all, but instead in Newburgh, a little village that's now more or less of a suburb, connected by highways and long corridors of shopping centers.

John Graze's house was in a neighborhood of tall trees and large houses spaced far apart. It had a few acres of lawn in front of it and a forest behind. It also had a wall going all around the property and a pair of iron-barred gates. The paint on the gates had begun to bubble and flake, and I could see the masonry crumbling in places along the wall. I sat idling in front of the closed gates for a second and wondered what I was supposed to do next. I didn't see a button or an intercom or anything, but it wouldn't be the first time I'd missed one of those. I was about to get out and search when the gates shuddered and began to grind inward on their own. As I drove through I kept an eye out for signs that a legendary metal musician lived here. Aside from a big, black car in the garage at the side of the house, there weren't any. No chanting cultists in robes, no frightened virgins running for their lives into the trees, just ragged grass and shrubs that looked like they'd been growing wild for quite some time.

Once I reached the house, I took the order out of the insulated carrier and ran up the front steps. I rang the bell and looked around. The place was big and old. It looked like it hadn't been painted in a while. It was the kind of place you might expect to find an elderly widow tottering around in, followed by a couple of loyal cats.

While I was daydreaming, the door opened, and there he was. John Graze himself, big as life. His hair had gone gray and it was cut short, but there was no doubt it was him. He still had the same eyes that I'd seen on the backs of the Left Hand Ritual albums. There was something else, too. He had a presence, an odd kind of energy, if I can use that phrase without sounding like a New Age goofball. Whatever it was, John Graze still had it, and it made me take a step backward and hold out the order at arm's length.

He paid me and took the bag. "Thanks," he said in a soft voice, then disappeared back inside his house. I stood on the doorstep for a few more seconds until my mind unfogged itself enough to move.

Back in the car, I reached under the passenger seat and dug out my camera. It was a Holga, a big, bulky plastic thing that I had bought at a flea market last year. Even when it was new, it would have been incredibly primitive. The focusing was guesswork, the shutter had exactly one speed, and as far as I could tell, the aperture switch was purely for decoration. But if you got everything right, you would end up with spooky, dreamy pictures of your subject that you couldn't get with any other camera. If you got it wrong, you would end up with blurry, off-kilter blobs that you'd try to make people think were on purpose. I carried it everywhere.

Yeah, I'm a camera guy. I forgot to mention that, didn't I? Well, I apologize in advance. I love cameras. I collect old cameras from garage sales and antique stores. I keep a shoebox full of film in the refrigerator. I own a light meter and a bunch of secondhand developing equipment.

So, to sum up: My name is Hal Hughes. I'm sixteen, I listen to heavy metal from the Eighties, I'm fascinated by cameras that normal people would throw away, and I'm a delivery boy. Impressive, right?

Sorry, ladies. I'm already taken.

I held the camera in my hands for a few seconds. I wanted to grab a shot of John Graze's house, but for some reason I couldn't bring myself to get out of the car and take it. I told myself that it was against my code of ethics as a delivery boy. I told myself that I didn't want him thinking the people from Jaya's were a bunch of nosy freaks. But that wasn't the real reason.

It was something about John Graze and those crazy rock star eyes. If someone had offered me a thousand dollars to get out of the car and take the picture right then, I don't think I could have done it. Instead, I stopped the car after the gates had closed behind me and took a picture of the gates themselves. The dark lines of the metalwork and the heavy stone posts made a nice composition, but that was just a consolation prize. I drove as fast as I could until the mansion was out of sight.

The next day I got off work at five, which gave me the chance to pick up my girlfriend from play practice. Every summer, all the high schools in the city school district pooled their resources to put on a production bigger than any of them could accomplish on their own. It was a big deal in Lamasco, and there was always some discussion about which schools had the most students in the cast, which teachers were in charge, and what kinds of biases this indicated on the parts of the director, the host school, and the school corporation as a whole.

This summer they were doing *Rent*. When I heard about it, I thought it was a little adventurous for a high school production, but I guess people reach a point where they've had enough of *My Fair Lady*. Macie Hart, who I'd been dating for a couple of months now, was playing Maureen. It seemed like a good part: big enough to be noticed, not big enough to feel responsible for the whole show. She was happy with it. This year they were rehearsing at Lamasco North High School, where Macie and I were going to be juniors in the fall. In a couple of weeks, they'd move everything over to the civic center, which was where the show would actually take place.

I slipped into the auditorium and sat in the back row. Up on stage, a couple of guys were singing through a song with the rehearsal pianist. They had it about three-quarters memorized and every so often had to glide over a lyric with hums and *la-las*. Behind them, a group was working on the choreography. Crew members scurried in various directions and some of the cast were catching a few unsupervised moments to talk, eat, or make out.

I sighed. I missed this. I had been in plays since I was in eighth grade, and I'd even had a little part in the all-city musical last year, but this summer I decided to take a break. Part of it was so I could try to earn some money, since camera gear wasn't cheap and my parents were only interested in subsidizing me up to a point. Also, I had come down with a killer case of stage fright right before the opening of *Grease*, North's spring musical, and the memories were still pretty vivid. When the time came to try out for the all-city, it felt like signing up for an extra dentist appointment. So I decided to skip it. Every time I came to pick Macie up and saw everyone else singing and performing, goofing around and having a good time, I wondered if I'd made the right decision.

But then, I reminded myself, if I didn't have a job I wouldn't have been able to afford the expensive medium-format film that my swell camera needed. I held up my Holga and scanned the auditorium through it. Things always look better through a viewfinder.

I saw a girl ducking out from behind the curtain. She was short, with red hair and what you might call an impressive figure. This was Macie. I waved. She hopped off the wing of the stage and I walked down to meet her. About halfway there, I caught sight of a gray-haired man sitting in the front row. At first, I thought it was just somebody's dad waiting for the rehearsal to be over. Then he turned and I froze.

It was John Graze.

"Hal!" Macie had reached where I was standing. She gave me a quick hug and took my hand, and for a second I forgot all about being startled by a retired heavy metal guy. She does that.

14

John Graze stood up and started walking over to us. Back in the day, he was rumored to have once bitten a chunk out of an interviewer's ear. Even now, dressed in nothing more frightening than a black t-shirt and gray pants, there was something about him that made me a little nervous.

"Very good job," he said to Macie. "You're coming along well." His voice was soft and rough, like he was trying to shake off some laryngitis, and there was just a tiny trace of the accent you sometimes hear in people who grew up in this area. I've tried to beat it out of my own voice ever since I could recognize it, but it's probably still there.

"Thanks," Macie said. "Singing over the band is harder than I thought it would be. It's a lot different than the piano."

John Graze smiled. He hadn't taken his eyes off Macie since they'd started talking. I couldn't help but notice this. To me, he looked like a snake staring across the pet shop at the hamster cage, but there's the slightest possibility that I might have been overreacting.

"Just make sure you hear yourself. That's the key. You can't think about them. You've got to think about you," he said.

I edged closer to Macie. I don't think he noticed.

"You'll be great. I can tell." That must have been all he wanted to say to her, because he released his hypnocobra vision and turned back to the stage, giving me a

15

quick nod along the way. It was probably nothing, just a simple acknowledgment that I existed, but it gave me the willies. It made me wonder if I'd irritated him in some way.

Did he remember me from yesterday? Had his order been cold? Impossible.

Out in the parking lot, I held the car door open for Macie. She was wearing a low-cut green top with lace around the neckline, and as she climbed in I took the opportunity to glance down the front of her shirt.

Oh, calm down. You would have done it, too. Well, you would have if you were me. We had only been dating since the spring musical at North, a couple of months ago, and I still got a little flutter in my stomach every time she smiled at me. The way I saw it, it would have been ungrateful *not* to look.

I started the car and took a quick picture while she checked her makeup in the mirror. She was used to it by this point and didn't even bother to tell me to cut it the hell out.

Once I'd pulled out of the parking lot, I asked her what in world John Graze, legendary rock recluse, had been doing at the rehearsal of a high school musical.

Her answer: "Who?"

I shook my head. Women.

"John Graze. The creepy guy who told you to hear yourself."

16

"Mr. Graze? Oh, right. It sounds different when you say his first name. Mr. Fanshaw—he's the drama teacher at Memorial, he's directing—said Mr. Graze was there to help out as a performance coach. And he's not creepy at all."

I still didn't understand why he was there in the first place. It seemed like a waste of the man's talents, like having Buzz Aldrin be the secretary for your model rocketry club.

"You know who he is, right?" I asked.

She shrugged.

"Am I the only person who knows this? Left Hand Ritual?" I prompted. "The heavy metal band? From back in the Eighties?"

"Like Poison?"

I cringed. "No, not like Poison. Not like Poison at all." Even though Macie's tastes ran more toward girls with squeaky voices singing over harpsichords and ukuleles, I was pretty sure she was just doing this to wind me up. "For a couple of years back then, Left Hand Ritual were the American Black Sabbath."

"That's good, right?"

Now I knew she was kidding. If she'd gotten anything from our relationship up to this point, it was a thorough knowledge of who Black Sabbath was.

"You know those little 'Parental Advisory' stickers you see on CDs and things?"

"Yeah."

"Well, Left Hand Ritual is one of the bands you can thank for that. They terrified people back then. There were all kinds of stories about them. Like they had to have a bucket of animal blood in the studio at all times. Or that nobody was allowed to speak to them at certain times of the day. Really bizarre stuff. For a while, everybody in the country knew them. Or knew their name, at least."

"What happened?"

"The band collapsed."

"Drugs?"

"No. Well, not *just* drugs. John Graze had some sort of a freakout. He got in a huge fight with the rest of the band on stage one night, then quit the group and disappeared. The band continued on for a while, but they had to replace him with two people: one to play bass, and one to write the lyrics and sing. They made two more albums without him. One was half-decent, and then the one after that was just terrible. As for John, nobody's seen much of him since."

"He seems nice now," Macie said. "He's got a lot of really good advice on how to sing."

"I wish I could get across how odd that is. Seriously, if you were going to make a guess at which Eighties metal musician would be least likely to help out with a high school musical, it would be John Graze." I hesitated for a moment. "Maybe that guy from Pentagram."

I pulled up in front of Macie's house. It was one of those big suburban jobs that had been built around the time John Graze was menacing the senators' wives on the Parents' Music Resource Council. I ran around to get Macie's door, then had her sit on the hood for a couple of goofy pinup-girl poses so I could burn off the rest of my film. The hood of a Civic isn't exactly prime pinup background, but we work with what we've got.

That night I hung up the blackout curtains in the basement bathroom and developed the roll. I'm still not an expert at developing film, but I can get images to show up most of the time, and I always feel like a genius when it happens. Like Prometheus. Like Cartier-Bresson. Like that dude at the Walgreens photo counter. It's an elite fraternity.

I wondered how the shots of Macie were going to turn out. More often than not, they were pretty spectacular. She had that natural ham quality that made her incapable of not striking a pose when someone pointed a camera at her.

I had box full of pictures of Macie. Part of that was because I simply loved taking pictures of her. She was beautiful and the camera loved her. But I had another reason, too. It was because of the of old Sterling Brewery.

The Sterling Brewery was this massive compound of brick buildings on Fulton Avenue, connected by walkways and dotted with smokestacks. It had been built in the nineteenth century, and it was a working brewery right up until some time in the Seventies. I saw it every week when my family drove across town to visit my cousins, and I always imagined what might be going on in those big, empty buildings that looked like visitors from another time. Were there ghosts? Did people live in them? What if they had a whole civilization hidden away in there, unknown to the rest of the world?

Then, one day, it wasn't there anymore. Just a bunch of yellow bulldozers and a mountain of bricks. Now it's a grassy lot with a billboard from some real estate developer on it. I can remember what it looked like, but I can't *see* it. I miss being able to see it. Even when I see a picture of it in a library book, it's not the same. It's not *my* picture, so it's not *my* Sterling Brewery.

When you take a picture of something (or some-*one* for that matter) it's real in a way that real life isn't. A picture stays the same. It's a frozen piece of time. It's yours. It's permanent.

That's why I take pictures of things. That's why I take pictures of her.

I finished the rinse and hung up the negatives to give them a wipedown with the squeegee. Everything looked all right. After I went over them with a blow dryer for a few minutes, I took them up to my room where I could feed them into the scanner. Is that cheating? Yeah, a little bit. But the truth is, I don't have any paper for the enlarger yet, and I was able to get the scanner with the film attachment secondhand from my mom's cousin, who has always been a gadget freak.

Once I was all done scanning, I printed them out on my cheap little photo printer. They turned out pretty well. Everything was in focus and more or less composed well. It's hard to ask for more than that. The roll started out with a couple of shots of Macie, then a soy sauce bottle on a table at Jaya's—a composition that was much more impressive in my mind than it turned out to be on film. Then some buildings in the neighborhood south of the restaurant. It used to be a pretty run-down area, but the city's trying to revitalize it as an arts district. Artists love Korean food, apparently, so I've spent a lot of time down there. As I said, it's good manners not to take pictures of the houses I deliver to, but there's always something interesting across the street or around the corner.

The only picture I screwed up was the one of John Graze's gate. I must have double-exposed it with something because there were all kinds of half-transparent shapes overlaid on top of the stone columns and the walls beside them. I held it up to my desk light to see if I could figure out what I'd doubled it with. Double exposures are one of my favorite things in film photography. If you're lucky, it can make a picture twice as strong as it would be otherwise. If you're not, it's just a mess.

As I looked closer, I realized that I was wrong. It wasn't a double exposure. Those half-dozen ghostly shapes were perfectly lined up with the contours of the walls and the posts. They weren't overlaid with the picture of the gate. They were a part of it.

I stared at the picture for a long time. I started to see more details in the ghostly shapes. They were the size of apes or deformed humans, with limbs that bent in the wrong direction as they scaled the wall. From the way they were facing, it looked to me like they were climbing over the wall and out of John Graze's estate.

As much as I told myself that it had to be a freak problem with the camera, the film, or the photographer, I couldn't quite believe that explanation. It really seemed like I had captured something that hadn't been visible when I pressed the shutter button.

To be honest, I had been listening to a ton of Left Hand Ritual in the past twenty-four hours and remembering all those gruesome old stories about the band, so I may have been predisposed to that conclusion. Invisible monsters from the lead singer's house seemed to fit right in with the band's reputation.

Whatever the explanation was, it was definitely weird. I put the picture in my desk drawer with the others. I'd take a look at it again later when I wasn't so freaked out.

2

The next evening, a summer thunderstorm blew up while I was at work. The sky darkened rapidly to a sinister blue-green and the rain began a few minutes later, just as the delivery orders started to come in. I sighed. You know that "neither wind nor snow nor whatever" stuff the post office always talks about? Well, it's the same for delivery boys.

By the time I loaded three orders into the back seat and pulled out of my parking spot, it was raining hard enough to make it tough to see. I wasn't worried, though. I had most of the city memorized, and could probably find the addresses blindfolded if I had to. I was born in Lamasco, as were my parents, and I had lived in the area all my life. It's not a bad place to be, really. Lamasco started out as a port city on the Ohio River, then switched to manufacturing during World War II, when they punched out waves of ships and planes, and the city has retained that old-fashioned heavy industry vibe ever since. In fact, I always half-expect to turn around one day and see everything in black and white. There are dozens of factories inside the city limits, all situated in the middle of the neighborhoods where their workers used to live. Not all of them are still open, but there are enough to keep things from feeling abandoned. I always got the feeling that the city could roll up its sleeves and build you a few thousand P-47 fighters again if it really felt like it.

I spent most of the evening driving around making deliveries. The weather didn't bother me, but I couldn't stop feeling nervous. After each delivery I found myself checking the back seat of the car for crouching maniacs. I suppose that's not too unusual, but the thing was, I *kept* checking. Every time I got in the car I could feel something behind me, peering out from some concealed place. Eventually, I started to think that if I could look in the rear-view mirror at the exact right time, I could see its shadowy form in a corner of the back seat, ready to spring at me when the time was right. This idea distracted me so much that I very nearly rear-ended a power company truck that had stopped to pull a fallen tree limb out of the road. After that, I did my best to keep my eyes where they belonged, but it wasn't easy.

Once I got back, Aunt Jaya called to me from the counter as I was drying my hair with an old apron. "Hal! Can you help close up tonight?"

"Sure. What happened to Nate?" Nate's one of the cooks who works a couple of nights each week. He's a huge guy, an Asian studies major at the University of

Lamasco, and is always asking Jaya about what life was like before she married my dad's brother and moved to America. The answer is always some version of "it was bad," followed by an instruction to go and do something menial.

"I let Nate go home early. He has cats."

"I see."

"He was worried about his cats and the thunder, so I told him to go home, make sure they were all right. The cats are good for him. They make him happy."

It was hard to argue with that, so I started wiping down the table and setting up the chairs while Jaya went in back to close up the kitchen. I had more or less gotten over my earlier nerves and wasn't thinking of much else besides whether I should mop the floor, and if any of the roads back to my house might have flooded. My family lives pretty far out, past the city/suburbs division and even past the division of suburbs and "urbs" of any kind. Macie and the rest of my friends think I live "out in the country," but it never seemed like that to me. I suppose they're right, though. No one else I hang out with ever has to deal with snowdrifts blocking the roads, packs of coyotes (I kid you not) or, like tonight, flash floods.

I decided to go ahead and mop the floor. Better to do it and impress Jaya than wait for her to tell me. I was going to end up doing it either way, so I might as well look good. I started at the front of the restaurant, where the big plate glass windows looked out on the street, and watched the rain make rushing sheets under the streetlights. Every minute or so, a flash of lightning would light up the row of buildings across from us: the insurance company, the music store, the bar and grill, and the big pawn shop owned by some friends of my parents. When the next flash came, I happened to be looking up from my mop just in time to see not only all that, but also a hunched shape pressed up against our window.

It's amazing what you can take in during the briefest of split seconds. At first I thought it was just a homeless guy trying to get out of the storm. Then the details started to sink in: Slippery, waxy skin, dark and purplish like an eggplant. Arms and legs that bent in the wrong places. Built like a combination of man, ape and insect.

The lightning flashed again. This time, I saw the face: Lidless eyes that bulged out like ping-pong balls. A circular mouth with jagged shark's teeth.

The thing put its hands on the glass and I swear I felt my heart stop in my chest. I knew beyond a doubt that I was going to die of fright right there and cause Jaya all kinds of problems with the health department. An instant later, there was another flash of lightning and the thing was gone.

For a minute, I mechanically pushed the mop around as my mind raced. I didn't see it, I told myself. It wasn't there. It was just some optical illusion. It didn't happen.

I bumped a table and knocked over the napkin holder, and nearly screamed from the noise. I took a deep breath. I looked at the window again, through half-closed eyes. The street was empty. Nothing was pressing its horrible face against the glass. Good. Keep cleaning.

By the time I finished, I was starting to feel more normal. I went to the kitchen and helped Jaya finish up in there. I didn't tell her what I saw—how could I?—but it was nice not to be alone. There was an unpleasant moment a little later when she let me out the back door and locked it behind me. Even though I told myself that the thing I saw couldn't have been real, I still imagined that it might at this moment be hiding in the alley, lying in wait for something as tender and delicious as me. I tiptoed out through the rain to my car, holding my keys so that they protruded from between my fingers like some ridiculous homemade ninja weapon, hunching my shoulders against the instant when it leaped out of the shadows at me.

I got away safely, but all the way home I had the same feeling as before, that there was something else in the car, watching me. Several miles out of the city, nearly home, I stopped at the intersection of Petersburg Road and Baseline Road. This intersection floods pretty quickly when it rains, and right then it was a black lake shining in the light from my headlights. I couldn't tell if the water was an inch deep or a foot deep. If I detoured, it would be fifteen more minutes alone with whatever I imagined to be in the back seat, so I hoped for the best and stepped on the gas. I was lucky. I got through the water without any problems and made it home. I was out of the car and halfway to the door before the engine completely stopped, but I made a point of slowing down before I went inside. My parents were still up watching TV, and I didn't want to have to answer questions.

Pretty soon, the panic had faded, driven away by my safe, comfortable house and my safe, comfortable parents. I changed clothes and had a sandwich. Before I went to bed, I took out the folder where I'd put yesterday's prints and pulled out the shot of John Graze's gate. It wasn't easy to be sure at first, since the things in the picture were all half-transparent, but it didn't take long to convince myself.

The thing that had stared at me through the window at Jaya's was identical to the creatures I had inadvertently photographed climbing over John Graze's wall.

The next evening, after I'd picked her up from rehearsal and we'd gone to see a movie, I showed the photo to Macie.

"What is this?" She held the picture in one hand and a coconut ice cream in the other. I'd taken her to Lloyd's, an ice cream shop across the street from school. The place has seen better days—judging by the decor, its heyday was some time in the Seventies—but it's the only place in town that serves coconut ice cream. Personally, I would choose coconut ice cream only if they were already out of the "burnt tire" and "grease trap" flavors, but Macie loved them. I wasn't sure if I was losing my mind or if I had really seen monsters, but either way the news was going to be a shock to her, so I figured she deserved her favorite treat.

"That's John Graze's front gate," I explained.

"Really, Hal? Is this what it's come to? You know, I bet I could get you his autograph if you wanted it."

"You're very funny. Look at the picture." I pointed. "What do you see?"

She squinted at the print. "Who are those guys? How did you do that?"

"I didn't do anything. They were there when I developed the picture. But not when I shot it."

She gave me a look and took another lick of her ice cream. "Come on."

"Seriously. They aren't camera tricks. I swear."

Macie frowned at me and I said, "That's not all."

I took a deep breath. "Look, I realize this is going to move me from 'took an odd photo' to 'possibly in need of psychiatric services,' but there's more. Those things in the picture? I saw one of them last night."

So I told her what had happened at Jaya's. I tried to keep the story plain, the way you would when describing a traffic accident to a police officer. Given the subject matter, though, it was hard not to make the whole thing sound like a ghost story. I got the feeling Macie was waiting for me to jump forward in the booth and shout

"Boo!" When I didn't, it took her a second to face up to the idea that I was being serious.

Macie's a practical girl, the daughter of a tax lawyer and an insurance accountant, and not the kind of person to believe in monsters. Neither am I, really, except that now I did.

She didn't say anything for a few long seconds. I got the feeling she was taking the time to choose her words carefully. Eventually, she said, "I know you've been listening to Mr. Graze's old band a lot, right? The imagery in those songs in pretty bizarre, isn't it? Maybe it sort of got into your head a little bit and..."

"I didn't imagine this," I said. I think I said it pretty calmly.

"I never said you did, Hal." She tapped the photograph. "This is a weird picture, no question about it. And I'm sure you saw something yesterday. I just think you may have... I don't know... *enhanced* it."

I was about to protest further, but then I stopped. What did I think was going to happen? Did I think she'd believe me if I just explained it one more time? All of a sudden I felt immense sympathy for every crackpot with a poorly-focused snapshot of a UFO, a half-effaced Bigfoot footprint, or welts from a heavy session of alien probing.

"Come with me." I stood up.

"To where?"

"I'll tell you when we're moving."

"You want to go look at his house, don't you?"

"Maybe," I admitted. Am I that transparent? Apparently so.

"Why?"

"I don't know. I understand if you don't believe me, but I can't let it go, and I can't think of anything else to do. Let's just go over there and see if we see anything strange. That's all. Please?"

She gave me a hard look, then finally nodded. "Okay. Let's go."

Once in the car, I leaned over for a quick kiss.

"Mmm, coconut," I said.

"I thought you hated coconut."

Another kiss. This one a little longer. "For some reason, it's growing on me." All on their own, my fingertips found themselves between the buttons of her shirt. "You know, we could just forget about this whole thing," I offered.

"If I believed that, I'd say yes." She gave me a half-serious shove. "Drive."

When we were on the road, she asked again, "We're just going to look, right?"

"Yeah."

"Really?" I could tell she'd been seized by the sudden fear that this might not be the best of ideas.

Instead of a reply, I pushed a Manilla Road tape into the cassette player. A few songs later, we pulled up to the front of John Graze's estate.

31

"This is where he lives?"

"Definitely." I declined to mention that, back before things got weird, I'd kept the delivery order with his address on it as a souvenir.

"It's gloomier than I expected," Macie said. "After getting to know him at rehearsals, I figured it would be something cheerier. Though I guess gloomy people can like musical theater, too."

"I'm not sure if that's true. Anyway, there's the wall and the gate from my picture. See anything?"

"No. Do you?" she asked in a cautious voice. I think she wasn't sure what to do if I said "yes."

"No." The longer we sat there, staring at a house and a wall, the more I felt like an idiot.

Finally, after another long minute of absolutely nothing, I started the car. "This was dumb," I said. I switched on the lights and pulled back onto the road. "I don't know what I was trying to prove. I guess I had the idea that if we got back to the spot, maybe you'd feel some of what I felt and, well, I don't know what was supposed to happen after that. I really hadn't thought that far. I'm sorry I dragged you out here."

I tried to see if she was annoyed or not, but she was looking in the opposite direction, out the window. For a second, we were on a stretch of high ground that let us see over the wall a little bit, into the woods behind his house.

Macie pointed. "What was that?"

An old fortress-like Methodist church quickly cut off our line of sight, but I got a glimpse of something that glowed with a bright yellow-orange light.

"Was that a fire?"

"Turn here!" she said.

I executed what felt like a movie-stuntman turn to get the car onto the narrow road that ran alongside the back edge of the woods.

In places, the belt of trees was thin enough to see his wall. As I drove, Macie scanned the view, in the hope of getting another look inside. "That was a huge bonfire," she said. "What do you think he's doing?"

The trees were broken up by a run-down antique store with dark windows and no cars in the gravel parking lot.

"Pull over there," Macie directed.

I stopped the car behind the store. When I shut off the engine, Macie looked at me for a second with a strange expression.

"Let's go see."

"Really?" I asked.

"I thought you wanted to know what he was doing."

"I thought you didn't," I said.

She shrugged. "Now I'm curious."

That's my girl. When Macie was at a girls-only summer camp in junior high, she and some friends had "borrowed" a canoe one night and paddled two miles across a lake in pitch darkness to visit the boys' camp on the opposite shore. When she wants to be, she's fearless.

We got out and started to creep through the trees, about as stealthily as you might expect from two people who spend most of their time indoors. The blue twilight was starting to deepen, but it was still light enough to see the outlines of each tree and keep us from tripping.

The wall was high. At least six feet and topped with little iron spear points that had fortunately rusted into softness with the passage of time. I gave her a boost up, and it is a testament to how focused I was on our adventure that I kept my hands where they needed to be while lifting. Most of the time.

"Camera!" She hissed down as she perched on top of the wall.

"Too dark! Sorry!" I whispered back. If I hadn't loaded it up with slow-speed, fine-grain film yesterday, I might have had a shot. As it was, it was pretty useless outside of direct sunlight.

I scrambled around and found a thick branch to lean against the wall and use as a step-up. Once I reached the top of the wall, I could see why Macie was so excited.

Behind his house, where most wealthy people might have had a swimming pool or an elaborate barbecue, John Graze had something that suggested all his band's moralizing critics had been pretty much on the nose. A gray stone boulder, ten feet tall or more, stood at the edge of the woods. A raging bonfire sat in front of it, contained in a round fire pit. As the flames threw light and shadow across the stone's face, it seemed to flicker in and out of visibility. One instant, it was gone, just a darkness among the trees. The next instant, it was back. The more I stared, the more it seemed that the stone had been roughly carved to resemble some massive crouching monster.

We sat there for a few moments, taking in Beelzebub's back yard, when a door opened at the back of the house and John Graze stepped out. He was barefoot, wearing a black t-shirt and gray pants. In one hand he held a glass of wine, in the other a rolled-up piece of canvas.

"Maybe we should go," I suggested.

He drained his glass and set it on the steps, then peeled off his shirt.

"In a minute," Macie said.

Whatever it was that spooky retired rock stars did, it agreed with him. Even with my beloved girlfriend ogling him, it was hard not to admit he was in damn good shape. Better shape than I was, without a doubt. If this was the end result of groupies, heroin, and Lucifer, I was going to have to change my career plans.

He faced the stone idol and spoke. I didn't think we'd be close enough to hear anything, but I caught every word.

"I have done what is required. I have arrived from the place I never left. I now come to you, father of fathers, key of keys, to claim what is deserved."

"Whoa," Macie said, before I shushed her. I didn't know what kind of acoustic trick made it sound like he was speaking right next to us, but the effect was unnerving and I hoped it didn't work both ways.

He knelt down and unrolled the canvas, which contained a kitchen knife the size of my forearm.

"Oh, my God," Macie said. The fact that it was just some ordinary thing, not a stage prop covered with gargoyles or goats' heads, made it even more frightening.

He held the knife in front of his chest with both hands and stared up at the stone idol's face. "I am the sturdy vessel, forged with deliberation and tested against the seven elements and against the nine divisions. I am capable of the highest attainment."

With that, he stepped into the fire.

He stood in the middle of the fire the way a normal person might stand in a wading pool. His clothes weren't even burning. He just stood there.

"I walk through the flames and I do not burn," he said to the idol. "I feel no heat. I feel no pain. I am the adept I claim to be."

Belatedly, I realized that a lot of this was word-for-word from the lyrics on *Black Aura*, Left Hand Ritual's second album.

He held his knife over his head. "I now tear the final seal, step outside of death and birth. I demonstrate that I deserve what I demand."

After he said that, he turned to his left and looked in our direction. I couldn't tell if he saw us or not, but I know that he smiled for half a second before he reversed his grip on the knife and plunged it into his stomach.

Macie drew in her breath with a sharp, terrified gasp and I yelped like a frightened animal. The shock of what he did hit us like a wave. We tumbled off of the wall and ran for my car.

We didn't say anything until we were halfway back to her house. Eventually, Macie spoke up. "Should we... call the police? The fire didn't hurt him. Maybe the knife didn't, either. Maybe he's fine."

I didn't really hear her, but her voice must have broken loose something in my mind. "I honestly did not expect that," I mumbled, more to myself than to her. "I figured he was like all the other guys who write really good devil music: pretty normal. I mean, that's what they do, right? They take all that darkness and weirdness and get it out through the music. When they're not performing, they play golf or collect spoons or run a vineyard. That's what they do, right? Right?"

"Hal, you're freaking out."

"Of course I'm freaking out. Freaking out is the only thing that makes sense. Ask anybody. 'Dear Abby, I just saw one of my musical heroes stab himself with a big

37

huge kitchen knife while standing in a pool of fire and praying to some gigantic Babylonian idol and I'm a little confused about what I should do next. Signed, Lost in Lamasco.' 'Dear Lost, you should be freaking the fuck out.' "

"Do you want me to drive?"

"I'm okay."

"I don't think that's true."

I turned off of Green River Road and into the maze of streets that led back to Macie's McMansion. When I stopped at her driveway, my heart was still thudding in my chest and my fingertips were tingling. The blue glow of the security light over the garage made Macie look luminous. I held her hand for a second. "I love you, you know that?"

She opened her door. "You're hysterical."

"Probably so."

3

I wasn't required at Jaya's until the afternoon, so I picked up Macie the next morning and drove her to rehearsal. She seemed a little nervous, and I suspected it wasn't because they were doing the blocking for her big song today. Would John Graze be missing? Would there be a sober announcement from the director that there had been a tragedy? The uncertainty was agonizing. I felt bad that Macie had to deal with this on top of rehearsing a tough song. I told myself that for our next date, we'd go out to dinner instead of peeking in on some devil-worshipper's ritual suicide.

When we opened the door to the auditorium, the first thing we saw was the man standing next to Mr. Fanshaw at the lip of the stage. It was John Graze. Big as life. Not a ghost. Macie wobbled and reached out for me. I gripped the edge of the railing.

Both of them turned and saw us standing frozen at the top of the auditorium. Mr. Fanshaw waved. "Macie! Come on down here!"

"What do we do?" she whispered to me.

"Do? Nothing, I guess."

"What do you mean?"

"Hey! Macie!" Mr. Fanshaw yelled.

"We can't do anything right now, in the middle of rehearsal. We don't even know for sure what happened last night," I said.

"So, do we pretend like everything's normal?" she asked.

"Macie Hart! Let's get started!" Mr. Fanshaw, like most drama teachers, had a pretty high tolerance for interpersonal crises and the whispered conversations that go with them, but there were limits.

"Go on," I said. "We'll talk about it later. It'll be all right."

"You think?"

"Yeah."

I wasn't sure she bought it, but she tottered down the steps toward the stage. John Graze detached himself from Mr. Fanshaw and moved in her direction, and I was filled with horror. But all he did was nod and smile as he passed. I was relieved. Then he walked right up to where I stood slack-jawed at the top of the aisle, and I was re-filled with horror.

"Hi there," he said.

I don't recall exactly what I said, but it wasn't anything worth remembering. I would have been inarticulate anyway, since I own all of his albums and there's a vintage poster of his band taped to my wall. But after what I'd seen last night, I could barely make a sound at all.

"Are you with her?" He pointed over to where Macie was leaning over the rehearsal piano, shoulder to shoulder with Micah Tomey, who plays Mark. They were taking instructions from Mr. Fanshaw and the pianist.

"Yeah," I said.

"Are you in the cast?"

I shook my head.

"The crew?"

Again, another shake. Mr. Suave, that's me.

"Just here to watch, huh?" He nodded thoughtfully. "That's cool. Always fun to watch sometimes." Down by the stage, Macie laughed and gave Micah a playful elbow, as if he'd told a mildly dirty joke. For a brief second I was resentful, as if she had no right to laugh at anything while I was up here being terrified. John Graze turned away from the stage to look down at me directly. He was really tall. I hadn't noticed that before. "Got to be careful, though. Sometimes you see things you can't unsee. You see things that make life hard. Even impossible. You know what I mean?"

I didn't respond right away. It was a little tough to think, what with the voice in my head screaming *"He knows! He knows! Run!"* over and over. When I finally did say something, it wasn't what either of us expected.

"Can I ask you a question?"

"Absolutely."

41

"Did you write the songs on *Homing Beacon*? I know it's got your name on the credits, but Tommy Jason always said they brought in Bob Daisley to do the lyrics."

I think he was more surprised than I was by the useless trivia question that leaped out of my panic-riddled brain. He actually took a step back, blinked at me, and seemed less threatening than he had been a second ago.

"Oh, you're a fan? Huh. Not many of those left. Well, *Homing Beacon*..." He thought back to the first album that Left Hand Ritual had done without him. "The way I remember it, we had some of the album tracked, and I had most of the lyrics written, before we went out on tour. Before things went bad. After that, I don't know for sure. I never spoke to the guys again. Bob probably came in to clean up the bass parts, and he must have written new lyrics for the new singer, because I'm sure they didn't use any of the ones I wrote. I imagine my name's listed on the album because they kept some of my music, even if they threw out the lyrics. I don't know for sure. I've never listened to the whole thing."

I nodded dumbly. For a brief, hopeful second I wondered if that little detour down memory lane, albeit a detour to one of the lowest points in his entire life, might have distracted him. It did not.

"Don't forget what I said before, all right?" He gave me a long, weird look. It felt like he was trying to see something behind me by looking straight through my head.

I backed away. "It was great meeting you, but I've got to get to work."

"I think you ought to get to work, then," he said, still staring.

Outside, I jumped into my car, checked the back seat, and cranked up the air conditioning. I tried to analyze what had just happened. I was pretty sure that the frontman from Left Hand Ritual had just threatened to kill me. Or possibly he was implying there might be something going on between Macie and Micah. But that idea was ridiculous, I told myself. Besides, I felt like I had more than enough justification to jump to the most sinister conclusion imaginable.

Still, as rattled as I was, there was a tiny part of me that felt disappointed in not getting his autograph.

Between Macie's rehearsals and my working at Jaya's, we didn't have a chance to talk before I was supposed to meet her at the ice rink that night. Macie's older sister Sandra skates in the local roller derby league, and tonight was their big match for the month. I dropped some ISO 3200 film into another of my old cameras, bought a ticket at the box office and went inside, glad to have something to take my mind off of ominous heavy metal guys and vague threats.

I took a few minutes to look around as I stood in line for my popcorn. The ice surface had been boarded over and a flat track had been laid down with various colors of tape. I took a deep breath of the humid, chilly air. It smelled like ice-making chemicals and locker rooms. I smiled.

A roller derby crowd was a great place to people-watch. You had big dudes in kilts, grandmas in pantsuits, guys with shaved heads and biker beards carrying their five-year-old daughters on their shoulders, sorority girls, families with kids straight out of the minivan, girls with Bettie Page haircuts and sleeve tattoos, everybody having a good time. It was a nice thing to be a part of.

I saw someone I knew sitting on the floor at the very edge of the track. This section was called the "suicide seats," so named because if one of the skaters lost their footing and wiped out, the safety padding was you. As exciting as it might sound to have a sweaty woman in ripped fishnets and spandex land in your lap, there was an equal chance of getting a quad skate straight in the jaw. The suicide seats were strictly for the rabid fans and the amateur sports photographers. Technically, you had to be over eighteen to sit down here, but they tended to look the other way if you didn't look litigious or too fragile.

"William!"

I had known William Cabell since eighth grade, when we both had ethical objections to dissecting a frog in science class and managed to pass off another lab group's pile of goo and organs as our own. William was another drama club guy, and had a part in the all-city musical as, I think, Miscellaneous Singing Bohemian #4.

"Whoa! What's that?" I asked as I sat down beside him and noticed the massive million-megapixel digital camera he held in his lap.

"It's my mom's." He must have seen me arch an eyebrow, because he quickly added, "And I'm using the manual setting, so just shut up, Hughes."

I was about to respond indignantly that I would never disparage another man's camera, but at that point the Lamasco Lambs skated out for their warm-up laps. William and I waved at Sandra as she went by, but she had her game face on and didn't notice us. Another great thing about roller derby? The skaters make up their own names. How can you not cheer for someone who calls herself "Josephine Bone-apart?" Or "Jane Ire?" Or "Affirmative Smacktion?" It's tremendous. Macie's sister skates under the name of "Ginny Dentata," which I had to look up.

"I'm supposed to meet Macie. Have you seen her?" I asked William, who was snapping away as the skaters flew past us.

He grunted. "A while ago. Over there somewhere. She was setting up." As family member, Macie usually got there early to help out.

I found her talking to an old guy in a black polo shirt with "security" printed on the front and "The Mad Chiropractor" on the back. Even the volunteers got nicknames.

Macie said goodbye to the old guy and we drifted off to find some seats at the top of the bleachers, where the view was best. I handed her the box of popcorn and we sat down. Nobody was paying attention to us, so now we had a chance to talk. Between my pictures, the thing in the rain, and what we both saw in John Graze's back yard, I think it was pretty clear we were wrapped up in something abnormal. The next question was, what did we do about it?

But then, before I could even clear my throat, she opened her bag and extracted a blue sheet of paper folded longways.

"Take a look at this," she said.

I recognized the paper right away. It was a take-out menu from Jaya's.

"Mr. Graze gave this to me."

I saw the little ripped spot at the top where it had been stapled to the takeout bag, and had a feeling that this was the very menu I'd given to him a few days ago.

"It was right when rehearsal was over. He just said he thought this was mine and walked off."

I frowned. What did it mean? Did he intend for Macie to show it to me?

"It gets better." She unfolded the menu and opened it up. "This is what was inside."

It was a strip of paper, long and narrow, about the size and shape of a bookmark. The paper was heavy and I could see little ridges and patterns in it, as if it had been made by hand. Along its length someone had painted a series of black, angular characters.

"What *is* that?"

"No idea," Macie said.

The writing looked half-familiar, like I'd seen something similar a long time ago. I picked it up to get a better look.

"Ow!"

"What's the matter?" Macie asked.

I blinked. "I don't know. All of a sudden, the thing felt... hot. Or something."

At that moment the Lambs, who had finished their warm-ups, made their official entry. The whole crowd stood up. The paper, which I'd been holding gingerly, slipped out of my fingers and nearly fluttered away behind the bleachers before Macie snapped it out of the air at the last second. Reflexes like a puma, that girl.

She folded it back into the menu and shoved it into her purse. There wasn't much point in trying to talk while everyone around us was cheering, so we shrugged and joined in. We cheered as the announcers ran through the names of the skaters, and cheered double-hard for Sandra. Sandra was like a version of Macie stretched out another foot and a half. She lined up in the middle of the pack with the rest of the blockers, whose job it was to clear a path for the tiny, wiry jammers to skate through and score.

Within minutes of the opening bell it was clear that the Lambs and their opponents, the Lexington Dethbutantes, were out for blood. They raced around the track, knocking each other into elbows, into hip checks, and into the fans. It was a rare two minutes that didn't see someone sulking to the penalty box then screaming encouragement as their teammates flew by.

I always watch roller derby with a mixture of bloodlust and concern. I love the hitting and I love the barely controlled chaos, but then I remember that I know one of the skaters out there and I hope that no one ends up getting hurt. I was thinking this when the pack came together around a corner, someone lost an edge, and all of a sudden there were skaters flying through the air.

It was the worst crash I had ever seen, far worse than the average wipeout. Skaters were lying on the track all over. As they started to pull themselves up, Macie grabbed my arm. It was Sandra. She lay sprawled on the boards in the dead-fish, boneless posture that tells you in an instant that something horrible has happened.

The referees quickly waved over to the sidelines and a couple of volunteers ran onto the track, including the old guy that Macie had been talking to earlier. They knelt over Sandra for a few seconds, then called for the stretcher. *Please move*, I thought to myself as I watched. *Please move.* They loaded Sandra onto the stretcher and I looked over at Macie, who was as pale as I'd ever seen her.

She was still clutching my arm like she was afraid of losing her balance.

They locked the stretcher and rolled Sandra off the track. She managed a weak wave while the crowd gave the customary standing ovation. Macie and I slid down from the bleachers and followed the medics.

They took Sandra by ambulance to Deaconess Hospital, where we caught up with Macie's parents. Macie looks like her mom, who is short, red-haired and apple-cheeked. Her dad is taller, with grey hair where he has any at all, and an expression that always makes him look like he's working out a calculus problem in his head. By this point, they'd already heard that Sandra had only suffered a bad concussion, and that nothing was broken. She was, though, responding sluggishly to some of the neurological tests and the hospital wanted to keep her under observation until she made more progress.

After Macie's mom explained all that to us, I pulled Macie aside and asked if I should leave and allow the Hart family to be by themselves for the time being. She shook her head and squeezed my hand, which I took to be a suggestion to stay.

A while later, after we'd had a couple of Cokes from the vending machine and split a pack of Chuckles, we had the chance to go see Sandra. Sandra was only allowed two visitors at a time and her parents had already been in, so there was a good chance that the stone-faced nurse with the clipboard wasn't going to give us a ton of time. We hurried.

Other than a neck brace and a couple of monitoring wires attached here and there, Sandra looked pretty healthy. I hesitated. What do you say to a person in intensive care, anyway? 'How's it going?' That just seems cruel.

Macie broke the ice by rushing forward and throwing her arms around her sister. "You scared me to death," she said.

"Ow."

Macie stepped back. "What happened to you out there?"

"I don't know," Sandra said. "I don't remember. Mom and Dad had to tell me about it. The doctors say that's normal, though. I may remember it soon. I may not."

"For a minute, I thought you were dead."

Sandra tried to shrug, but winced. "Do you know what time it is? Did we win? God, those Chicago girls were monsters."

"Lexington," I volunteered.

"Hi, Hal."

"How are you feeling, Sandra? I think you're the first sports injury I've ever seen up close." I held up my camera, which I'd been carrying unconsciously for a couple of hours now. "You mind?"

"Go ahead." She put on her best stoic, injured-warrior expression and I took a couple of shots. The whole Hart family is full of performers. Even their parents won't keep a normal face if they see a camera. I suppose it's possible that they're just sick of having me take their pictures.

"I actually don't feel all that bad," Sandra said. "I don't think they gave me anything stronger than aspirin, so that's got to be a good sign." She sighed and closed her eyes.

Macie folded her arms. "You're going to make sure you don't skate for a while, right? I've read about concussions, and they're supposed to last for a lot longer than..."

I had been mesmerized by the blinking lights of the brain-monitor thing, so I only turned around when Macie trailed off. Then I saw what was wrong.

Sometimes when I'm playing with photos on the computer I try to create a fake double exposure by layering one shot on top of another, then adjusting the transparency of the top photo until I get a result I like. As strange as it sounds, that was how Sandra looked: like someone had overlaid another image on top of hers and was oscillating the two back and forth.

In this case, the other image was a bulging-eyed, insect-skinned thing. It was the same kind of thing I'd seen in my picture of John Graze's gate, then seen again through Jaya's window.

51

"Do you see that?" I hissed to Macie.

"What's happening?"

"I don't know." My mouth felt dry and it was hard to make the words form. The beeping and hissing of the medical equipment seemed incredibly loud.

We stood there frozen for I don't know how long, probably not more than a minute, while Sandra and the purplish monster-thing cycled in and out of existence. What made it worse was that the transformations were agonizingly erratic. Sandra would be there for the space of two heartbeats, then the thing for one, then Sandra would be return for a longer time and we would start to think it was all over, then she would shift back to the thing again.

Once, when the thing had been there for a very long time, it moved. It turned its head, featureless except for those giant eyes, toward us and opened its mouth. It had no tongue, but gnashed its triangular shark-teeth together hungrily.

It sees us, I thought. *It knows we're here.*

Then, with a ragged gasp, it faded back into Sandra. She stayed there for five seconds, ten, fifteen, longer than she ever had since this all started. Her eyes were closed. What was going to happen now? As we stood staring at her, the door opened and both of us jumped about a foot.

"I'm sorry, but it's time to go," said the nurse as she came in with a paper cup in each hand. "She needs her— Oh, she's asleep already? Well, let me make sure that everything's all right."

Macie and I backed out of the room. I felt that we ought to do something: warn the nurse or just ask her to watch Sandra for a while to see if she noticed any monster-related symptoms. But I was way too shocked to come up with the right words to say. Besides, I had a feeling that what we saw was meant for us only.

Macie asked her parents if I could drive her home and we walked out to my car feeling numb and unreal, like after a visit to the dentist when you're still half full of Novocain and nitrous oxide.

I started the car and we sat there for a second. Finally, Macie said, "What the hell was that?"

"That… was what I saw at Jaya's."

"But why? Why Sandra? Where did it come from? What does it have to do with her?"

I didn't say anything. Instead, I looked down at her purse, which held the folded-up takeout menu and the strange strip of paper from John Graze.

4

I drove Macie back to her house. Halfway there, she sighed and seemed to sink into the seat a little.

"So, this is real," she said. "There are really wizards. There are really monsters. They're out to get us."

There wasn't anything I could do but nod.

"What do you think happened to Sandra?"

"I don't know," I said. "Maybe it was some kind of warning. Or maybe he's trying to get to us through her."

Macie laughed. "You know, this is actually kind of liberating. We don't have to keep trying to convince each other that we saw what we saw. We know how things really are. And we're in it together."

"When you put it that way, it doesn't sound so bad."

She squeezed my hand.

"We'll have to think up a reason for you to drop out of the musical," I said. "I bet nobody would say anything if you did. You know, because of Sandra and everything."

She shook her head. "No. Forget it."

I didn't press the issue. Even as I'd said it, I knew she wouldn't agree. It was unthinkable. It doesn't matter if your performance coach is a sorcerer and your sister is turning into a monster. The show must go on.

"I'll stay away from Mr. Graze as much as I can," Macie said.

I slowed down as we moved through the mall traffic on Green River Road. "That's a good idea. We don't know how his magic spells work, but I bet it's related to that strip of paper. So don't let him give you anything else. Don't let him touch you."

"I wasn't planning on it."

"You still have the paper, right? We can try to figure out what that writing is supposed to mean."

"Then what?"

"I don't know. But it may give us some kind of clue. Can you hang on to it until I get off work tomorrow?"

Unsurprisingly, work took forever and everybody was twice as irritating as usual. The tips were barely spare change, Jaya was a taskmaster, Nate couldn't cook to save his life, every customer left an unholy mess at their table, and there was this one chunky guy with a beard who made a plate of mixed vegetables last for more than two hours. He spent most of that time staring at me. That was what it felt like, anyway. I probably stared at him just as much, checking to see if he was going to turn into an eggplant-skinned monster and chase me around the restaurant. I even made sure to get a look at him in the mirror behind the counter, just in case his reflection revealed his true form.

Now that I think about it, I probably know why the guy kept staring at me. He thought I was insane.

Things got worse when I went to pick up Macie after rehearsal. She wasn't there. It was fifteen long minutes, checking among the dissipating knots of actors, while I elevated steadily from irritation to concern to panic, before my phone buzzed. It was her. Her parents had collected her early to go to the hospital, where her sister was being discharged. She didn't know when they'd be done. I told her I would start working on our research project and let her know what I found.

My plan, such as it was, was to hit the library and hope I stumbled onto something good. I didn't see any other way to go about it. As Macie and I had seen, this was real magic, and something inside told me I would have better luck with dusty old books than with the internet. Fortunately, I knew exactly where to go for dusty old books.

Willard Library sits on the south end of First Avenue, along with an Army surplus store, an old church, a Mexican restaurant, a row of historic houses, the hospital where my grandfather was a surgeon in the 1950s, and a biker bar. Basically, it's my favorite street in the entire world. Someday, I'm going to stock up with film, pick my best camera, and just walk up and down First Avenue taking pictures all day.

The library was built in 1885 and claims to be the oldest public library in the state. It's got a tower and all sorts of gingerbread architectural details on the outside: little carved stone owls inside of oak-leaf wreaths and stern cherubs that look down on you as you climb the limestone steps. I love it. It's even got a ghost, though I tried not to think about that now.

I pulled open the doors and stopped for a second in the entryway, like I always do. A heavy wooden staircase led up to the second floor and down to the basement. The walls had huge paintings of nineteenth-century Lamasco dignitaries and, for some reason, George Washington. I took a deep breath. Oil soap and old wood and books. If any place in the city was going to have books on magic, sorcery, or curses, this was it. I turned left into the main reading room and headed for the stacks. Sadly, they didn't have an old-fashioned card catalog like I thought they should, so I fired up the single tiny catalog computer and started searching.

I didn't know the best way to begin, but I couldn't really wander up to the reference librarian and say, "Hi, I think my girlfriend's drama teacher is some kind of a wizard or a necromancer or something and I'd like to know more about the subject. Could you point me to the right shelf?" Instead, I looked up everything under "Magic" and tried to weed out all the books on card tricks and sleight of hand.

I copied down catalog numbers from the hazy computer screen. When I closed my session and turned away, something caught my eye over by the circulation desk. A guy was sitting there. At first I had just taken him for another library patron hunched over a book, but then something clicked in my mind and I looked again. I had seen him before. It was the guy from the restaurant, the one who had taken two hours to eat a plate of mixed vegetables.

I tried to shrug it off as a coincidence, but the fact that he was staring at me again didn't help any. I moved a couple of rows over and started to look up my numbers in the occult section. There wasn't a huge amount of books on the subject. Willard Library has a massive collection of art books and genealogy archives, and everything else fits in where it can. Usually, though, the books they had were good ones. I felt confident I could find something.

My first choice was a hardcover book called *The Magicians Speak*. It was written in 1968, and its cover was a web of magical-looking diagrams in a spectrum of psychedelic colors. As I flipped through it, I found a bunch of tables and charts inside. Some of them even had symbols that looked like what I'd seen on Macie's strip of paper. This one was obviously worth checking out, so I put it under my arm and reached for the next book. Then I felt somebody standing next to me.

"Reading up on the occult, huh?" said a voice.

It was the guy. I didn't know how he had managed to sneak up on me, but all of a sudden there he was, twelve inches behind my right shoulder. The man took up a lot of space. He was pretty big, much taller than me, and heavyset. He had a brown beard, and wore thick-lensed glasses with clear plastic frames. His button-up plaid shirt was tucked into his khakis.

He smiled at me like we were already friends, then turned his head sideways to read the title of the book under my arm.

"That's a good one," he said. He smelled like mildew and mint. "That's not bad at all. But you've really got to watch out—"

I didn't hear the rest, as I was rapidly backing away with the exaggerated casualness of the thoroughly weirded out. I hurried into the next aisle, then took the book over to the circulation desk, where I hoped the presence of the librarian would prevent any further bizarre behavior.

I handed over the book and my library card, and while the librarian did her thing with the computer I looked over my shoulder. The guy was gone. Willard Library is not a huge place, so I could get a look at the whole of the first floor by just taking a couple of steps. When I did so, it confirmed my suspicion. He wasn't there. He had simply vanished.

I stumbled out of the library and into the parking lot, trying to look in all directions at once. I was so sure that the big bearded guy or the phantom monsters were about to ambush me that it was an actual surprise when I reached my car unmolested. As I drove home I listened to the classical music station. That's not really my thing, but all the tapes I had in the car—Pentagram, Axewitch, Mercyful Fate, and a Left Hand Ritual bootleg—were not the kinds of music that were going to make me feel less paranoid.

I turned onto Diamond Avenue and thought about the bearded guy. What could he have wanted? Had he followed me all the way from Jaya's? My thoughts spiraled off into increasingly bizarre directions. Did he know John Graze? Hell, was he John Graze himself, in some sort of magical disguise? What if he was one of the monsters, wearing the skin that he had peeled off of some other innocent victim? What I got home, would he be sitting on my porch, still wearing that bland, friendly smile and holding an axe in one hand?

I had to admit, though, that the guy hadn't actually done anything weird except look at me and stand too close. Now that I thought about it, someone his size was almost always going to stand too close if he was crowded into Willard Library's narrow aisles with another person. Then I started to feel bad. A perfectly valid alternative to the scary, supernatural explanation formed in my mind: Wasn't it more likely that he was just a guy with no social skills who had recognized me from the restaurant and tried to be friendly? And then I, already keyed up from the past couple of days, had flipped out for no reason. I winced as I followed this train of thought. Maybe this guy, a shy loner, was right now cursing himself for screwing up another interaction with a fellow human being. I could have made the guy's day with just a smile and a nod, but instead I acted like a jackass. Now I really felt bad. I deserved to have John Graze's monsters eat me.

That night I went to a late movie with William. Macie was busy with her family, and I hadn't hung out with William in a long time. William was a good friend of Macie's old boyfriend, and he also knew the girl who I had been dating pretty seriously until a few months ago, when Macie and I found each other backstage at *Grease* rehearsals. William had gotten pretty sick of being the go-between and the complaint department during the rough couple of weeks after Carlos and Julie found out what Macie and I were doing. If I could go back and do it again, I would have handled things differently. But, as it was, I did a bad job and got people mad at me, including William.

Over time, things got better. You can't stay mad at your friends forever, even when they act like idiots. I was just glad that we could go and see movies again. I had forgotten that cinema-going was such a different experience when you weren't trying to feel up the person next to you.

There was nothing that either of us particularly wanted to see, so we decided on some vampire movie that looked like the least bad thing on the marquee. Maybe it would even give me some ideas on how to deal with a supernatural menace like John Graze. At this point, I didn't even know what John Graze was trying to do, so it was hard to figure out how to respond to him.

I bought a popcorn and some malted milk balls. William got Twizzlers and a pickle as large as his forearm. The concession stand has a tank full of giant pickles, and it's the most disgusting thing I've ever seen. I think William only gets them because he knows they appall me.

We took a pair of seats in the back. Once we were situated, I asked, "So, how's the musical going?" As if it were an idle question.

"Everybody's really good. It's kind of intimidating."

"How's John Graze?"

"Mr. Graze? Okay, I guess. He doesn't spend a whole lot of time talking to the chorus."

"I mean, has he done anything weird?"

"Why do you ask?"

Because, William, I'm pretty sure that Mr. Graze the performance coach is actually an evil wizard. I'd like to know if he's been bewitching the cast somehow.

Instead, I said, "No reason."

"Um-hm." William's tone suggested he knew I wasn't telling the whole story, but if I wasn't going to explain myself right away, he could be patient until I did. That boy can pack a lot of expression into two syllables.

While I opened my box of malted milk balls, William dug into his pocket and took out his phone.

"I don't know if I should show you this or not," he said, while scrolling through his texts, finding one, and showing it to me.

It was from Micah Tomey. Micah was a year ahead of us at North, and was playing Mark in the musical. He was good, too. I can act, and I can sing a little, which is usually good enough to get by, but when I watch Micah, I can tell that he's on another level. Most of the rest of us are acting in high school plays. Micah is an *actor*. You don't realize how big of a difference this is until you see it in front of you.

This was his text to William: "Is Macie dating anyone?"

The bastard.

"I told him she was, but it was just you, so he should definitely give it a shot."

"Dick." I knew he was kidding.

"Seriously, it probably doesn't mean anything," William said. "But I thought I ought to let you know."

"Thanks a lot."

William bit the end off his pickle, sucked out the juice, and the house lights went down.

The movie was terrible. Within fifteen minutes, it became clear that this was no monster movie. It was a love story. If I had thought I could defeat John Graze with the power of love, the movie would have been very helpful. As it was, it was a waste of ninety minutes.

After the movie, when William and I split up in the parking lot, I thought I saw a big guy with a beard a few rows over, standing by his open car door and watching me go past. I didn't try to get a closer look, but instead hurried to my car and drove off. I took the long way home, just to make sure I wasn't followed.

I dug into *The Magicians Speak* in earnest as soon as I got home. I had flipped through it before going to the movie, but now I started to really study the thing. The book was a history of witchcraft and sorcery, and one of the author's main ideas was that witches and sorcerers, or whatever else you wanted to call them, communicated by means of secret coded messages that they passed to each other or sometimes hid in plain sight. This had been going on throughout history, supposedly. The author felt that the plays of Shakespeare were primarily a giant message board for communication between the members of the secret coven who actually wrote them. This was where I started to get concerned that I was reading pure craziness.

But there, among the lunacy, was the thing that had made me check out the book in the first place: a table of big, angular letters that looked a lot like the ones I had seen on the strip of paper. According to the book, the letters were called "runes," an ancient system of writing that went all the way back to prehistoric times in Europe. The book showed pictures of runes carved into the sides of stone monoliths and along the edges of Viking shields. Each rune, it seemed, stood for a letter, just like a regular alphabet, but they each had a special magical meaning, too.

Then I hit something that made me sit up in bed:

> In the early days of primitive sorcery, the power of the written word was valued above all else. The runes, both singly and in complex conjunction with each other, were seen to have explicit power in the phenomenal world. A rune of storm could bring relief from drought. A rune of thorn could blight an otherwise healthy crop and choke it to death with brambles. Used in combination, runes could carry curses and death, not only for the man wise enough to apprehend their meaning, but to anyone who came in contact with them.

For a second I hoped the next section of the book would begin with something along the lines of "And here are the steps to take when afflicted by magical runes like the ones I've just described." No luck. But at least I had something now. A foot in the door, so to speak. I stuck a scrap from a film carton in the book to mark my place and drew a star next to the important parts. (Lightly. In pencil. It was a library book. I'm not a barbarian.)

I went to bed feeling optimistic. The book had a pretty big bibliography, and there was a chance I could learn more about the runes from some of the books it listed. That night, I dreamed that everyone I knew had become a vampire while I wasn't paying attention and I could save them by taking their picture, but all my film cameras were broken and all I had left was the crappy little camera on my phone, which was a problem because everyone knew that vampires didn't show up on digital.

I woke up early the next morning and was downstairs before my dad left for work. As he read the paper, I dug through the bread box and found a blueberry bagel that had been forgotten about for a long time. I tapped it on the counter. How stale was too stale?

"Hello, son."

"Hi, Dad." I sawed the bagel in half and shoved it into the toaster.

He reached for a pen on the counter. My dad reads the paper in the same way every day: straight through, front to back, then the crossword puzzle, which he does in pen before he leaves for work.

"How's it going with Jaya?" he asked. Dad's brother is Jaya's husband, which is how I got the job.

"Not too bad. I'm getting some great pictures when I'm out on deliveries."

"That's good. She's going to miss you when school starts back up again. She says you're the only teenager she's ever hired who didn't make her teeth hurt."

"Really?" I felt an idiotic surge of pride at that.

"Macie's in the musical this summer, isn't she? How's she doing?"

"Pretty well, so she tells me. Kind of having a problem with one of the assistant directors, though."

"There's always drama in the drama club, I imagine."

"You could say that," I said.

Dad returned to his crossword, and I retrieved my bagel and resumed my slog through *The Magicians Speak*. As nice as it had been to have a regular conversation about regular things, I had work to do. I began to write down some notes.

My first delivery of the day was only a few blocks south of the restaurant, in a neighborhood that's been hovering between "arts district" and "slum" for as long as I can remember. Right in the center of it was the old Alhambra Theater, a beautiful building with a vaguely Moroccan facade and its name down the side in big letters that used to light up. There were boards over the windows. It had started out as a movie theater back in the nineteen-twenties, but was used less and less as the neighborhood fell apart. If you can believe what you read on the internet, the Alhambra hosted some legendary underground punk and metal shows in the Seventies and Eighties. But soon after that, it was closed for good. Every so often there would be reports about someone getting a grant for renovation or finding a potential buyer who promised to restore it, but nothing ever seemed to get done. Even though I was a sucker for a picturesquely run-down building, I always hoped that someone would put the place back in shape again. It was too nice-looking just to let it sit and rot.

I was thinking of the posters for those underground rock shows, and how damn creative the flyer-making guys had been with just a pair of scissors and glue, when I reached my address. It was a big, old house, built back in the day when you had to have a whole wing just for the servants. Somebody must have been renovating it, because it was half covered with scaffolding and much of the dirty yellow siding had been pulled off. Just as I rang the bell, I realized that I'd left my zippered bag of small bills and change on the front seat of the car. I was glancing over toward the car as the door opened, and when I turned back I saw something that I hadn't expected to see.

All I could take in at first was the shiny, waxy eggplant skin, then those round expressionless eyes like the eyes of a creepy stuffed toy, and finally the teeth. It was just like what I had seen through the window at Jaya's. An instant later it was on top of me.

My head bounced against the wooden porch and the thing crouched on my chest. I remember being surprised that it didn't have any smell. I would have accepted anything, from that acid smell of a squashed bug to the stench of rotten meat, but there was nothing. Just the scent of seaweed-wrapped rice that had fallen out of my delivery bag. To my shocked mind, it was all still unreal. Then it sunk its teeth into my shoulder.

It hurt. I can't lie about that. It felt like a ring of tiny needles chewing into my shoulder, but it wasn't agonizing. In fact, as my vision started to get black around the edges, then fade out altogether, I hardly noticed the pain. I hardly noticed anything at all.

5

I heard shouting from somewhere. Why was someone shouting? All I wanted to do was sleep. Why couldn't anyone let me sleep? What was wrong with this blanket? But the yelling didn't stop. Instead, it got louder and closer, and was joined by the sound of heavy footsteps.

I blinked. I was lying on somebody's porch. My shoulder hurt like I'd just ripped something under the skin. And kneeling next to me on the porch was the big bearded guy from the restaurant and the library. He was wearing a faded Incredible Hulk t-shirt that made me feel sad for some reason that I couldn't articulate. I might have been in shock.

"Are you all right?" he asked.

"That'll be seventeen sixty-five," I replied, which was the first thing that came to mind. My thoughts began to get a little clearer. This guy couldn't have called in the order, I told myself. I heard him run up here from the sidewalk. He ran up here when—

I thrashed around like a lizard, looking for the thing that had attacked me.

"What just happened?" I asked.

"Can you stand?" He helped me up.

As I got my balance again, he waved his fingers in my face, a weird fluttering motion that could have been a complicated pattern or could have been completely random.

"What are you doing?"

"Can you still see me?" He was watching me closely, with an expression on his face that I couldn't read.

"Of course I can see you."

"You have to go," he said.

"Why?" I asked, then followed his glance as he looked through the open front door and into the house. We could see down the entryway and into the kitchen at the far end. There was something on the floor there. A sprawled shape in a yellow polo shirt and shorts. Unmoving.

"Oh, my God," I said.

The guy scooped up the spilled food and dumped it back into the bag. He scrunched down the top and handed it to me. He looked up and down the street, which was deserted except for an old man in the distance, walking a fluffy white dog and coming this way.

"I'll explain later, but not now. You have to go."

"Who are you?" I demanded.

"Just go. *Please.*"

Something in the guy's tone convinced me. I stumbled to my car and drove off. In the rearview mirror, I saw him go into the house and close the door behind him. I felt like my mind had stopped working. I drove around for a while until I started to think a little more clearly. I stopped at a corner and threw the delivery order in a trash can. When I got back to Jaya's I crept into the bathroom and pulled off my shirt. There was nothing there. Nothing much, at least. If I stared, I could see a faint red circle going around my shoulder, but that was it. There weren't even any rips or tears in my shirt. How was that possible? I rolled my shoulder around. It didn't hurt anymore, but it didn't feel quite right, either. It was like that for the rest of the day. Sometimes it felt a little cold, and sometimes a little hot, and sometimes I was just "aware" of it in a strange way. I tried not to think about it, which wasn't too hard.

At first, my thoughts were taken up by the images of two faces. One was the glistening, bulging-eyed monster, and the other was the bearded guy in the Incredible Hulk shirt, staring at me with a mix of worry and fear.

Then a strange thing happened. As I worked the rest of my shift, those thoughts faded into the background noise of my mind. It was like what happens when you have a bad dream: no matter how upsetting and gruesome the dream was, and how much you'd like to keep the dream fresh in your mind, just so you can figure out why it scared you so much, the details fade away as the day goes on, like an instant photo in reverse.

I kept thinking that I ought to be panicking. I ought to be running down the street screaming for the police or an exorcist or something. Not only had I seen one of those creatures again, but it had actually attacked me, pouncing on me like I was a gazelle at a waterhole. But then I would get distracted by an order to deliver or a table to bus, and the next time I thought about it, it wouldn't seem like such a big deal. At one point, I actually caught myself thinking, "If that had really happened to me, I'd be freaking out right now." That gave me a weird feeling, but twenty minutes later I couldn't remember why the idea had bothered me.

That night, I went over to see Macie and found Sandra out in the driveway, shooting baskets. She stared at me as I walked up to the house.

"How are you feeling?" I asked.

"Pretty good. The doctors say they've never seen anyone recover so fast."

"Seriously?"

"Yeah. They still want me to go back for a bunch of tests, though. Brain scans and stuff."

"Well..." I wanted to say something witty here, but I drew a blank. I finished up instead with a lame "Good luck, okay?"

"Think fast!" Sandra fired the basketball at my head. Acting on instinct, I slapped at the ball with just enough force to divert it away from my face, which was as graceful as it sounds. It bounced off the ridiculous garden gnome in their flower bed and rolled to a stop on the gravel.

Sandra chuckled as she picked up the ball. "Macie's inside," she said, and launched another shot at the hoop over the garage door.

I watched her for a second. Sandra had always intimidated me a little bit, what with her being my girlfriend's older sister and everything, and I had the impression that she didn't think I was quite right. When you act in musicals and take people's pictures all the time, you get that occasionally, so I had never thought too much about it. But throwing a basketball at my head seemed cruel. Maybe it was a side effect of the brain injury. Maybe I was being oversensitive. I told myself to let it go.

Inside, after a few minutes of small talk with her parents, Macie and I went upstairs to watch a movie in her room. This may have been another reason why Sandra was annoyed by me. As Macie tells it, Sandra would never have gotten away with a boy in her room in a million years. Some of that was because she tended to date guys with tattoos, trucker hats, and none of my natural charm. The larger part, though, was that Macie just got away with a whole lot more than Sandra ever did. Sandra, in her turn, had gotten away with a lot more than their eldest sister Jane, who, to hear Macie tell it, was brought up like a nun. It was the classic situation: By the time Mr.

and Mrs. Hart got to Macie, they either knew that super-strict parenting was not as important as they thought it was, or they had just ceased to give a rat's ass. Whatever the case, I was the one who benefitted, so as far as I was concerned the system was great.

We were propped up on a nest of pillows on the floor in front of her bed, watching something ridiculous on her little TV. Outside, it had started to rain. I felt nervous and unsettled, like I was in the wrong place at the wrong time. But why would I be in a weird mood? Then I remembered.

Should I tell her about what had happened earlier today? About the monster-thing that had bitten me and the odd guy who had helped me escape? Of course I should. But I didn't. I didn't want to think about it, and I didn't want to relive it, so I distracted myself by leaning in and kissing the back of Macie's neck.

I ran my hand down to her shoulder, the same place where I had been bitten. All of a sudden, I felt hot. Was I getting a fever?

"Did you notice anything about Sandra when you saw her?" Macie asked, which snapped me back to the present moment.

"I don't know. What do you mean?"

"She's been acting different since she got home from the hospital. That's supposed to be normal for a bad concussion, but I think it's something more than that."

"How so?"

"That's the problem. I can't really say what it is. She's just *different*."

"Well…" I thought about bringing up how Sandra had just thrown a basketball at my head, but Macie continued on before I could find the words.

"You know what I mean, Hal. Ever since that time in the hospital, ever since she… *changed*, she hasn't been the same person. She's different now."

I wanted to agree with her, but I couldn't say anything. My attention kept drifting to the back of her neck. I kissed her again. I could taste her orange-blossom perfume. She made a little sound and pushed up closer to me. I realized that, despite what she'd said, maybe she was looking for a few minutes where she didn't have to think about what was wrong with her sister.

All of a sudden we were on the floor, pressed tightly against each other, kissing like we owed each other money. Okay, that's a bad analogy. But you know what I mean. Everything, from the sound of the TV to the rain against the windows, sounded like it was coming from a long way away, distant and echoey and soft.

Things got stranger after that. My vision, when I had my eyes open, had a dark haze around the edges. The darkness expanded until all I could see were the impressions of things rather than the things themselves. I saw Macie as if I were looking down at her from a height, through a thick fog. There was something about her expression that I knew I ought to recognize, but I didn't.

More kissing. It was a struggle to keep kissing her, but I couldn't understand why. Still, I knew I had to fight to keep doing it. I was on top of her, and it was an effort to stay there, but I had to. Something kept pushing at my hands, but I couldn't see what. I could hardly see anything, but I didn't care and couldn't think about it. I heard something through the roar of blood in my ears. A ripping sound. Then Macie's face again, with an expression I'd never seen before. It startled me for a second and all of a sudden I felt like I was falling and everything went black.

I blinked and it was gone. The black fog, the roaring in my ears, all of it was gone. I was on the floor in Macie's room, on my back, propped up on one elbow, with a throbbing hot pain at the base of my skull. I must have hit my head on one of the hexagon-sided free weights half-stowed beneath her dresser. I was nearly on the other side of the room. How did I get all the way over here? I looked up at Macie. She was kneeling with her back to the wall and staring at me with huge eyes. She held her powder blue t-shirt together with one hand. It had been torn open down the front. From one side, part of her bra hung loose, its front clasp twisted off.

I did that?

"What the hell's wrong with you?" she panted.

"What?" Not the best response, I know, but I was honestly clueless as to what had just happened.

"Get out," she said.

"What did I do?"

Macie pulled her ripped shirt tighter around herself. She kept staring at me, not like I'd gotten hormone-poisoned and stupidly pushed things too far, but in some different way that was frightening to see. Like she was afraid of me. Like she didn't know what to expect from me, but it wasn't going to be anything good. Like the trusted family pet had suddenly snapped at her.

"You... changed," she said.

"I don't know what happened. I just..." Then I understood what she meant. I licked my lips. I could taste Macie's lip gloss and something else, something metallic. Blood. I thought back to the creature that had sunk its teeth into my shoulder, and left a bite-mark that I couldn't see. I knew what had happened.

"Just for a second, I saw the same thing we saw in the hospital," she said.

I felt sick, but I knew she was right. The spell, the curse, whatever the hell you wanted to call it, had gotten to me, too.

"You wouldn't listen to me. You wouldn't stop." Macie glanced up at the door. "Thank God nobody heard us."

"You'd better put something else on." I waved vaguely at her shirt.

She hopped up and started to pull things out of her dresser.

"I'm so sorry," I said.

"Hal, what happened to you?" She was putting on a new bra and shirt, facing away from me. I wondered how far I could lean to try to catch her reflection in the mirror and still look natural. Apparently, I *was* still me.

I explained the events from earlier today: the delivery, the bite, the bearded guy. She listened without saying a word.

"So I don't know what happened to me, just like I don't know what happened to Sandra," I said in conclusion. "I understand if you want to stay away from me. I'm going to figure out what's happening, but I don't want you to be around if you think you're in danger. I don't want anything to happen to you."

Macie didn't say anything for a second. Then she shook her head. "No. We'll do it together. We're in this together, Hal."

She took my hand, and I felt all the tension drain out of me. I had been lying a moment ago. There was no way I could try to do this all by myself.

"We'll learn what Mr. Graze is doing," she said. "We'll follow him. We'll talk to people who know him. We'll spy. We'll break into his car. Into his house, if we have to. We'll figure it out. We'll make him stop. I don't know how, but we will."

I squeezed her hand. "We will."

I was still a little woozy from having assaulted my girlfriend while the victim of demonic possession, so I decided to call it a night early. We crept downstairs, past

79

where her parents were watching TV in the den. We hoped that if we crept casually enough, her parents wouldn't notice that Macie was wearing a different shirt. As we kissed goodbye on the porch I thought I felt her pull back a little. I didn't say anything and I didn't want to think about what that meant.

The next morning, when I went down to the kitchen, I saw the stacked-up newspaper where my dad had left it on the counter. As I poured milk on a bowl of corn flakes a small article on the bottom corner of the front page caught my eye.

Assault in Haynie's Corner Shocks Residents

Andrew Price, longtime resident of the Haynie's Corner Arts District, was attacked yesterday afternoon in a daytime assault that authorities are calling a likely result of an interrupted burglary.

Price, 37, owner of the Fountain Gallery and a member of the Parrett Street improvement board, was knocked unconscious in his home at 709 First Street yesterday afternoon. Price had returned from a shopping trip and appeared to surprise a burglar in his home.

"I remember setting down my bags, then going to pick up the phone because it was ringing. After that, everything went black," Price said.

Though Price did not see his assailant, neighbors reported seeing two men running from the house at separate times, soon after the assault. One man, described as heavyset and bearded, wearing a pale shirt and jeans, drove off in a dark-colored car. The other, smaller and light-haired, possibly a juvenile, left in a second car, which the witness described as possibly being yellow.

There was more after that, quotes from the police department warning neighbors to be vigilant, and statistics showing that this part of town was still relatively safe and much improved from the bad old days. Quotes from the neighbors saying how terrible it all was. Stuff like that. I didn't read the rest too closely. Once I hit "smaller and light-haired, possibly a juvenile," I wasn't able to focus on much else. However, two things flooded my mind with relief: One, I was thankful that the old guy with the poodle hadn't gotten a good look—my car is actually green. Two, I had forgotten to put that stupid magnetic signboard with "Jaya's Authentic Foods" on the roof of my car yesterday.

I drank some orange juice, which tasted bitter. Then I got dressed and tried to start my day. I thought about taking some pictures, which was what I usually did when I was nervous, but I knew I wouldn't be able to concentrate. My mind was filled with vegetable-skinned monsters and, I realized, very possibly run by them as well.

Later on, I gave Macie a call. It was an awkward conversation at first, because I think she was trying to figure out if she was talking to Jekyll or Hyde. I could understand that. After a few minutes of boyfriend-girlfriend talk, I told her about the newspaper article. She hadn't seen it, and judging by her shocked reply, I think it made the whole affair seem even more real. Not only were we dealing the forces of darkness, but now the law was involved as well.

"Do you mind if I come over?" I asked. I picked up *The Magicians Speak*, which had a bunch of post-it notes sticking out of the sides, from the table next to my bed. "There are some more things I wanted to show you."

"Umm… Sure. I have to leave in a couple hours, though. Some of us are getting together at North to run through the choreography."

"Who's going to be there?" I asked. You know, casually.

"I don't know. Just some of the principals. We want to make sure everything's right, and we're running out of time."

"I see," I said

"Can you come over right away?"

As I drove to Macie's house, I kept looking up at the sky. I knew it was my imagination, but I couldn't help noticing how some of the cloud formations looked a lot like faces. I could hear the wind pick up as we sat in her room and I showed her the pages I'd marked.

"Look at these." I turned to the page that had the list of runes, along with descriptions of what each of them meant in the coded language of the magicians.

"You've still got that paper he gave you, right? If we can find the runes he used, maybe we can figure out what he's trying to do. And if we know that, maybe we can see how to stop him."

"*If* this book is right," Macie said as she opened a drawer and dug around inside. "I mean, the writer could have just been making stuff up."

"It's the only lead we have. If this book is a fake, I don't want to know."

Macie took out the folded-up menu from Jaya's and carefully unfolded it. I saw the strip of pale yellow paper lying in the center of the blue menu for a second. Then, as if a stray draft had picked it up, it flew into the air. It fluttered, twisting, to the window, where it smashed itself flat like a moth hitting a car windshield.

We stared at it. It hung there, the writing side facing away from us, plastered against the window. My first thought was that some freak breeze from a partially-closed window in the hall had done it. Then the paper burst into flame, and I admitted I was wrong.

It burned quickly, with a multi-colored flame that reminded me of Fourth of July fireworks, and it was gone before we could dash across the room to grab at it. There was nothing left but a fine patch of bluish ash on the windowsill.

"That… was not normal," Macie said.

"We're lucky it didn't set the curtains on fire."

"I don't think it was meant to." Macie ran her finger down the place on the window where the runes had stuck. "Do you think the curse is, you know, over?"

"I don't know. I don't feel any different." A thick mass of cloud passed over the sun, throwing Macie's back yard into deep shadow. Under the big sugar maple in the back, I halfway thought I saw something standing there, looking up at us. I stepped away from the window.

"Either way, the book was right, though," I said. I had only seen the strip of paper for a few seconds, but it had been long enough. I pointed to the table in *The Magicians Speak*. "It was the same runes."

"Well, that's something, at least." Macie checked the clock on her desk. "I've got to get to rehearsal. Want to come with?"

"Sure." Generally, watching someone else rehearse is as exciting as watching someone else lift weights or play video games. Which is to say, stupendously boring. But I wanted to spend time with her, so I went along.

It was only an informal rehearsal for the dozen or so cast members who weren't happy with their songs and choreography yet, so none of the teachers, including John Graze, were there. Neither were any members of the "orchestra." (I'm sorry, but any orchestra that includes a pimply dude with a flying-V guitar and some sullen-looking girl playing a Jerry Only skull-head bass is going to get quotation marks put around its name.) Music was provided today by a student pianist, who I actually dated for a few months as freshman. I was a little surprised that there were so many people here for an optional rehearsal, but the summer musicals usually tended to attract the ones who care very much about getting it right. Maybe this was another explanation for why I decided to be a delivery boy instead of an actor this summer.

I skulked around in the first few rows of the auditorium with the other boyfriends and girlfriends who were making the sacrifice. I took a few pictures with my Canonet, partly because I wanted to practice some low-light shots without the flash, and partly because I had to do something. I took my best guess at the lighting conditions, then slouched down in my seat so I could put my feet up on the seat backs in front of me and make a sort of tripod out of my knees. From there I took pictures of whoever drifted far enough downstage to make a good composition. Eventually, I used up the entire roll. I was amazed to realize that I'd forgotten to bring another. Walking around with an unloaded camera makes me feel naked. However, this is only a problem in the summer, since as soon as it gets cool enough for a jacket I'm never too far from an extra roll of film, my light meter, or on days when things are really out of hand, an entire spare camera.

To keep from sitting and fidgeting, I hopped up and started to prowl around the amphitheater. The production was just about ready to leave its rehearsal home and move to the Civic Center, where the actual performances would be. Disassembled scenery flats were leaning against the side of the stage, and there were a dozen boxes lined up by the auditorium doorway, full of things like sheet music and binders marked "lighting plans." One of the boxes contained stacks of printed programs. I picked one up and leafed through it, stepping into the hall to get better light. I looked through the thumbnail-sized pictures of the cast and noted with pride that Macie was by far the prettiest one there. After the cast, there were the pictures and biographies of the adults and teachers involved. There was Mr. Fanshaw, trying to look like a responsible adult and not a drama teacher. After him, I saw the music director, the choreographer, and the set designer.

I stopped. There was John Graze. Not a publicity photo from his long-haired, blood-drinking days, but something taken recently, showing him in a black sweater, looking coolly at the camera. If it hadn't been for the eyes, he probably would have seemed like a normal person. I read the short biographical paragraph next to the photo:

John Graze (performance coach) is a Lamasco native, and was a member of a well-known rock band in the 1980s. Now retired, Mr. Graze keeps busy as a private music tutor and a member of the Alhambra Theater board.

I read that again. The Alhambra. That old boarded-up theater downtown. The one that, conveniently enough, was located just around the corner from where that supernatural thing had attacked me yesterday. I stared at the program with unfocused eyes while the refrain from "Seasons of Love" drifted up from the stage. I thought two things: First, I'd be perfectly happy if I never, ever heard that song again. Second, what better place for an occultist to hang out than some abandoned building dressed up like a fake Moroccan palace? All of a sudden I was very curious.

I slipped back into the auditorium. Some of the cast were going over the steps for a song that Macie wasn't in, so she was sitting in the front row, watching. I crept up and kissed the top of her head.

She flinched as if stung by a wasp and nearly decked me before she realized who I was. Given the circumstances, I probably should have expected that.

"God! Sorry, Hal."

"No problem. Hey, do you think you can get a ride home with someone else? There are a few things I want to check out."

"*Things*? Like with, you know, *him*?"

I nodded.

Macie was about to interrogate me further, but Micah Tomey, the guy playing Mark, hopped down from the stage, took her hand, and led her away. They were on to a new song now.

"Yeah, okay," was all she had time to tell me before bounding onto the stage. I wished there had been time for a real kiss before I had to leave. On the way out, watching her tango with Micah, I felt like I needed one.

The Alhambra theater is at the intersection of a couple of oddly-angled streets. On one side, there's an art gallery separated by a wide alley. On the other side of the Alhambra was an upscale tool-rental shop and another art gallery. It was, after all, the Arts District. In case you're wondering, the organic foods co-op was a block over and the coffee house was a couple of blocks to the north.

Personally, I loved this little spot. It always seemed interesting, so much so that I tended to detour through it whenever I had to deliver food to any address around the area. I parked by the fountain across the street from the Alhambra and got out. I made a point of not looking up the street to the house where the thing had attacked me.

The theater was dark. The rows of light bulbs that crawled along its marquee had been out for years, and the box office windows were boarded up with plywood. I made sure no one was looking, then I casually tried the handles on the main doors. Locked. Of course. No surprise there. There had to be lots of other entrances, though. Since I was here, I ought to try them all.

I walked around to the wide alley between the theater and the art gallery. Someone had installed concrete planters here, and the place looked less like an alley and more like a walkway or a plaza. I walked with my hands in my pockets and whistled to myself in an attempt to be inconspicuous. A second later, I realized I was whistling "Kneel Before," a Left Hand Ritual song. I immediately switched to a medley from *Grease*.

I'd left my camera in the car, which was a shame. If I'd had it, and someone stopped me, I could have said I was just scouting around for some good pictures. I imagined that a picturesque neighborhood like this, with lots of semi-distressed old buildings, must get a ton of obnoxious people with cameras wandering around and annoying people.

The side door had "Alhambra Staff Only" stenciled on it. I pulled the handle idly, as a curious person with no ulterior motive might. No luck. I was about to try it again, even harder, when a big, black car, parked on the street past the vacant lot behind the theater, caught my eye.

I'm not generally much of a car guy, but something was telling me that this car was important.

Then I remembered. It was the car that had been parked in John Graze's garage when I first went to deliver his order. It was John Graze's car. John Graze was here. It wasn't any one of the hundreds of other people who must also own a big, black car in a city of one hundred thousand people. It was him. I could tell. I rubbed my shoulder, which was suddenly aching in a dull way, and went to see if there was another entrance.

There was. In a weedy loading area at the back of the theater, under a rusting fire escape, was another steel door. As I got closer, I could see that it wasn't completely shut. It looked like it hadn't latched properly the last time someone had gone through it. I took one more look around, then carefully nudged the door open and slipped inside.

Once inside, I was hit by the oddest old-new smell. There was mildew and rot, which made me think of abandoned clothes and decaying crushed-velvet seats and curtains falling to ruin. But there were also the scents of fresh-cut plywood and new paint and some sort of stripping chemicals that I recognized from my dad's workshop. It smelled like they were trying to renovate the place, but they hadn't won the battle yet.

When my eyes had adjusted to the shadows, I saw I was in a short hall that led to the backstage area of the theater. Like all theaters, the backstage was essentially a deathtrap, filled with precarious arrangements of beams and cables, all waiting to be tripped over.

I shuffled forward and tried my best to avoid anything that might fall over or collapse if I touched it. After a few steps, I heard a voice coming from the stage. I froze. The voice mumbled something, there was a pause, then it said something else. I inched closer, and soon I could hear that the voice was making some sort of chant, alternating a call and response with itself. I reached the wings. From there I could see the stage, which was a little bit smaller than the stage at my high school. Beyond the stage, the house lights were on and I could see rows of seats, upholstered in stained, dark red fabric. A couple of small spotlights shined on the stage from the wings. In the center of the stage, where the spotlights hit, was a series of tall white candles arranged in a wide circle. In the middle of that circle stood John Graze.

John Graze, retired heavy metal guy, private music tutor, performance coach for the summer high school all-city musical, member of the Alhambra Theater board, and all-out fucking warlock, stood barefoot and shirtless inside the candles, spinning around in a ritual dance.

As he moved, he continued the sing-song chant. I could catch little bits and pieces of English, but most of it I couldn't understand at all.

"Tet an Ausar! Anet hrak suten sutenui!"

"Maat! Ram Tepek Maat!"

"Marduk destroyer! *Marduk re-maker!*"

"Tenesh Marduk! *Tenesh Ashtoroth!*"

I felt like I ought to do something. I felt like I should jump out, knock down his candles, and shout "Gotcha!" But I didn't move. Eventually the chant wound down in a mixture of humming and babbling, and John

Graze sank almost to the floor, hugging his knees and resting on the soles of his feet. Just when I thought he might blow out his candles and walk away, he stood up from his crouch, stretched, and looked right at where I was hiding.

"Come here," he said.

I had a better idea. I was going to run away. But just as I was about to turn, I stepped out from behind the ratty curtain and onto the stage. I didn't step out against my will. Instead, for a crucial half-second I honestly felt that stepping onto the stage was a good idea. I wanted to do it. Then I understood, and my blood ran cold. I did it because he made me do it. So this was magic, I thought. Not just flashing lights and rabbits in hats. Not even scary monsters that jumped out at you. Magic was control. And I was controlled.

"You're just not going to go away, are you?" John Graze asked.

I didn't say anything. I couldn't say anything. He stood in the middle of his candles and stared at me, the way you might look at some big stupid bug that wandered into the kitchen and you can't decide whether to scoop him up with a piece of paper and throw him outside, or just squash him with your shoe.

"Well, at least you're a fan. You can consider that little performance a peek at what our fourth album might have sounded like. Tommy and Phil would have fought like hell, of course. They always complained when we did anything that didn't make us sound like Whitesnake. I would have recorded it without them, but..." He shrugged. "I lost my voice."

I knew what he was talking about. This was all part of the legend of Left Hand Ritual. Halfway through the tour for *Controller of the Real*, their third album, John Graze and the rest of the band had gotten into a huge fight on stage, and the band disintegrated. Their fourth album, which was halfway finished, was reworked with a new singer, new lyrics, a new bass player, and a dumber title—*Homing Beacon* instead of *Lords of Air and Darkness*. John Graze set off on a solo career. Almost immediately after, he lost his voice. Some people said it was due to throat cancer, and others said it was just a cover for massive drug problems. Either way, he disappeared from the music scene, and society in general, for years afterward.

This was not the time to be curious, but I couldn't help myself. I found myself slurring out the words, "What happened?"

He seemed surprised to hear me talk. "I don't know," he said. "Maybe it was stress. We were on the road all the time back then, and fighting a lot. Or maybe it was the drugs." His eyes looked past me for a second, as if he was seeing something far away. "There were so many drugs. And I was doing other things, too. Maybe I called down something that didn't want to be called, and it took revenge on the thing I loved the most. All I know for sure is that suddenly I couldn't sing anymore."

He gestured to the candles, and I could see words written in chalk, snaking around them, in a language I didn't recognize. "But I had other things to keep me busy," he said.

"I did miss the music. But I missed the audience more. Did you know that I played one of my first shows right here at the Alhambra? That's when I got hooked. There's nothing like an audience. All those people screaming for you in the darkness. It's a hard thing to let go of."

I nodded. It was a little easier to move than it had been before.

He looked around the dusty, half-renovated theater and smiled to himself, as if this was exactly where he wanted to be. That was when I started to hear noises from all over the theater. It sounded like the chattering and buzzing of bats, and the crackle of dried insect shells. When I looked out past the stage I saw movement. It was the creatures. There were hundreds of them, all with blank white eyes and circular, howling mouths. They stood shoulder-to-shoulder, pressed together like a rest-less festival crowd. They weren't standing on the seats, but instead moved through them, like they were super-imposed on the scene. They all stared up at us.

"This is my great work," John Graze said. "My time in Left Hand Ritual gave me the money and the power, and ever since then I have devoted myself to making this come about. I have repeated my rituals over and over through the years, and they have worn a soft place between this world and another. These servants have already begun to walk from there to here. Soon they will attach themselves to people in this world. Some have already begun. When it is finished, the people will look the same. They will act the same, more or less. But they will be *mine*."

The translucent things were surging around in front of the stage now, but they went no farther. I shuffled a few inches backward. The grip of John Graze's magic had loosened as he kept talking. But the truth was, I wanted to hear what else he had to say.

"Then there's you." He sighed. "When you keep poking around in places you're not supposed to be, bad things happen to you. Believe me, I know."

"I didn't mean to," I said. It was a lame excuse, but I felt like I had to offer one.

"It doesn't matter. It's who you are. All of you. All those kids in the musical. So much energy. So much curiosity. So much emotion. You feel things so deeply, with such violence." He laughed. "Twenty years ago, I never would have guessed where I was going to find the energy I needed, but it's working. It's working better than I ever hoped."

He ran his hands through his hair and smiled, like he was congratulating himself on his good fortune.

"Some of them are just unbelievable. Your red-haired girl, for example. Macie Hart. Horrible voice. Great body. And such a talent for spreading chaos. Everyone around her ends up doing things they never expected themselves to do. You've seen it yourself, haven't you? Some people are like lenses. They have an amazing ability to focus and enlarge people's energy. I can use her for quite a bit. You, however..."

He reached behind the candles and picked up a foot-long knife with a curved blade and a complicated handle. This looked far more like a wizard's dagger than the big kitchen knife he'd stabbed himself with earlier.

"Blood is life," he said as he gestured to the half-transparent creatures at the lip of the stage. "Both for them and for us. Though in different ways, of course."

He stepped out from inside the candles and to-ward me. As he did so, one leg of his pants brushed against a candle and caused it to wobble. As it swayed, I felt the magical grip loosen even more. I knew somehow that when it stopped moving the grip would return, so I struggled as hard as I could and an instant later I was stumbling through the dim backstage area, crashing into every discarded ladder and paint can between here and the exit.

I was sure that John Graze was going to stab me in the back as I ran, or at the very least tackle me, but there was no pursuit. Instead, I heard him shout "No!" then a string of half-angry, half-frightened words I didn't understand. They reminded me of a lion tamer barking orders at his animals. Maybe the vegetable-insect creatures weren't entirely on his side after all. *Good*, I thought. I hoped they gnawed him to bits.

There was a sound behind me like a small thunderclap, but I had reached the back door by then, and wasn't going to turn around. I charged through the door and into the fresh air. The wind had picked up again since I went inside, and I took a second to stand and cool off, overcome with relief. Then I started running. If I'd been thinking clearly, I would have just run to my car, but once you've seen an inter-dimensional army of monsters and been threatened with death, and the poaching of your girlfriend, by a guy whose poster used to be on your wall, it tends to do bad things to your judgment.

I ran across the street, then veered off in another direction when I saw John Graze's sinister black car parked there. I sprinted past the community art center and around the corner, only to stop dead when I saw the house where the creature had attacked me. At that instant I was absolutely convinced that it was still waiting there, and would finish the job if I got any closer.

Back down the street the other way. Soon I saw the fountain crouching in front of me like some big metal bug. I realized that I had frantically run in a large square and would soon be back at my car.

That's when the doors of a parked car opened up and half a dozen guys jumped me.

6

At the time, it felt like half a dozen guys. Once they had thrown me in the back seat of their powder-blue station wagon and we were moving down the street, I realized that there had only been two of them. They were sitting on either side of me, while two more guys sat up front.

I felt a little nauseous. My residual panic after escaping from John Graze had soured into sickness, and the smell in the overcrowded station wagon wasn't helping. It seemed like a combination of cologne, sweat and old food. On top of that, I recognized the person in the front passenger seat. It was the big bearded guy with glasses, the one who had been following me for the past few days. He squirmed around to look at me over the seat back, then held up a white cloth about the size of a handkerchief. There was a red design embroidered on the front of it: a kind of cup with Greek letters over it, all encircled by a sun with pointed rays.

"Be bound, warlock!" he said from behind the cloth.

"From sun to sun and moon to moon, we bind and confuse thee," said the one on my left, a wiry guy in a plaid shirt.

"In all spheres and all vibrations, we bind thee," said the one on the right. He had a little goatee and round shoulders. He also had two Greek letters drawn in chalk on his forehead.

"I don't think he's bound," said the guy with the plaid shirt.

"I thought you said this would bind him!" piped up the driver, who sounded a little frantic.

"Watch his hands!" said the guy with the goatee.

The bearded guy in the passenger seat had draped the white cloth over his head. I could feel his glare right through the fabric.

"I see something, but it's... I don't know," he said from under the cloth. "This doesn't seem right."

"Look," I volunteered, "just let me out of the car, and I swear I won't tell anybody anything."

The plaid shirt guy barked at me, "Who do you work for?"

"Jaya Hughes!"

This must not have been what they were expecting. They all glared at me in silence for a few seconds. Slowly, they began to exchange looks with each other.

"In the name of the nine aeons and the consort of spheres, I oblige you to answer truthfully," said the voice from under the cloth. "Tell us your true name."

"Hal Hughes. Harold Montgomery Hughes."

"Something moved," he said, still under the cloth. He sounded for all the world like one of those scientists in monster movies that stares at the radar display and calls out the latest developments as the giant monster makes its inexorable way toward the heroes' bunker.

"So we're right?" asked the driver. "He's one of Graze's creatures?"

"John Graze? You guys know John Graze?" They ignored me.

The head under the cloth shook. "I don't think so, but there's something there for sure."

"Should we kill him?"

"Not in the car!" said the driver.

The bearded guy pulled the cloth off of his head. "No, we should not kill him," he said, apparently disgusted that one of his buddies had even suggested that.

"It has to be the Expulsion Working. Grab his head."

Immediately, two pairs of hands ratcheted my head around until the bearded guy could stare into my eyes.

"Sorry about this, Hal," he said, before beginning to chant in a rumbling tone.

I heard a few words in a strange language, then there was a heavy pain at the back of my neck. The next thing I remember was standing unsteadily under a tree in front of Willard Library, soaked with sweat, a little dizzy, and all alone. I sat down on the bench for a second to think things through. Any passing library patron would think I had lost my mind, but that didn't matter. As a matter of fact, I *had* lost my mind. Part of it, anyway. How I had gotten from the weird guys' car to here was a complete blank. I checked my watch. An hour was gone, missing completely from my memory. I also had no explanation for why my neck was so sore, starting right at the place where the skull joined the spine, then radiating over to where I had been bitten. At first, I figured that one of the guys in the car had whacked me in the back of the head, but then I realized that my neck and shoulder didn't actually hurt. I gently stretched them. They were sore, sure, but it was the good kind of sore, the way it feels when you're finally able to pop a joint that's been bothering you all day. I sat up a little straighter, which was when I noticed that my car had been moved to the Willard parking lot.

The door was unlocked and the keys were behind the sun visor. On the driver's seat was a white business card. I stared at it as I sat in the car and let the air conditioner run. The card read "St. Mark's Methodist Church," which was totally not what I was expecting. It showed an address on the east side of Washington Street and had information about phone numbers and service times. I turned the card over. On the back, someone had drawn two swords crossed over a pointy-rayed sun, all in green ink. There was a date and time underneath that.

Six-thirty. Tomorrow. The penmanship was impressive. It was almost calligraphy, in fact. I smelled the card. Sweat and cologne. Just like the guys in the station wagon.

As I drove away I thought about whether I should show up at the church tomorrow and what it might mean if I did. I didn't even notice until later that all the dread and panic from my meeting with John Graze was gone. I was still concerned, sure, but for some reason I was a lot less hopeless than I had been. As a matter of fact, I felt pretty good.

Did I end up going? Of course I did. I got off work and tried to scrub off the kimchee smell in the bathroom of the little apartment that Jaya keeps upstairs above the restaurant. No one knows why she has it, and when asked she always says "I'm going to rent that out one of these days," but she never does. I always assumed that's where she drags unappreciative restaurant critics and works them over with foam-covered pipes and pliers wrapped with electrical tape, but who knows for sure? The only personal touch I've ever seen up there, a half-empty bottle of thirty-year-old Korean mouthwash, has not given me any clues.

I drove to Macie's house to pick her up before I went to St. Mark's. It would have been easier for her to meet me at the restaurant, but I felt apprehensive about introducing her to my aunt. Jaya is what you might call old-fashioned, so much so that I always wonder if she's planning an arranged marriage for her son, my poor cousin Chris. Because of this, I'm always afraid she'll fix an enormous "welcome to the family" banquet if I ever bring the same girl to the restaurant more than twice.

I had given Macie a short, three-sentence description of what had happened yesterday, along the lines of "I saw John Graze doing some ritual on the Alhambra stage. I left the theater and ran into a bunch of strange guys. They gave me a card from St. Mark's." I told her I'd explain more when I could figure out what to say. After I had woken up under the tree, everything before that felt unreal, like it had been a vivid but utterly bizarre dream. I couldn't figure out the right way to describe what had happened.

When I got to her house, Macie was out the door before I could even put the car into park. She let herself in and we kissed, not as long as I would have liked.

"You smell nice," I said. I'm a total sucker for perfume. Good, bad, cheap, expensive, I do not care. If it came in a sparkly bottle and you're wearing it, there's a good chance I'm going to end up doing whatever you ask.

"Thanks. I thought it would go well with the kimchee."

I got out of Macie's subdivision and onto Oak Hill Road. It's the longest and slowest way to get back into town, but it's a much nicer drive. I'll take hills, farmhouses, trees, and ten extra minutes over gas stations and billboards every time.

"Hey, can I tell you something?" I asked.

"Sure."

"About the other night. When I kind of went... Well, 'nuts' isn't the right word, and I hate to say 'possessed'..."

"That's all right. I know what you mean."

"Thanks for sticking with me. I mean it. Are we still okay?"

"Yeah. I think we are."

That was not exactly the fevered declaration that I had been hoping for, but I was more than willing to take what I could get. As long as she didn't feel like she had to walk around with a Taser in her purse, I was fine. Of course, I hadn't looked in her purse recently. Maybe there was one.

"How's the show going?" I asked, changing the subject.

"We're getting close to dress rehearsals. It's stressful. I don't think we're ready."

"Everyone thinks that."

"There's Sandra, too. Something's still wrong. The doctor says she's recovering, but I don't know. There's a lot of weird stuff, Hal."

She shifted slightly to watch the houses go by. "Stuff you wouldn't notice if you weren't looking for it. She used to like pears, but now she can't stand the sight of them. She can't bear light. Even the light in the living room is too much, she says."

"Well, that doesn't sound too unusual for—"

"That's not the worst part. Last night she was standing at the bathroom sink, brushing her teeth. I wanted to go in to get my allergy pills, but as soon as I saw her there, I froze. I could not make myself walk in there with her. I knew, and I don't know how, but I knew that if I walked in there and saw her reflection, it wouldn't be her. What do you think that means?"

I didn't say anything. What it meant was that we were running out of time, and I still hadn't told her all that I knew. John Graze was using magic to bring his creatures from some other world into our own, and they were starting to take people over. If we didn't do something, Sandra wouldn't be the last.

St. Mark's Methodist Church was in a part of town that was mostly residential, little brick houses built before the second world war. It was old enough that the trees in the yards had had time to grow and mature. As far as I was concerned, this was what separated a neighborhood from a suburb: If the trees were taller than the houses, then you lived in an actual neighborhood. We passed a couple of funeral homes, a middle school, and a little garden center before we got to the church. It was just a few minutes after six-thirty and the light was starting to get golden, the way it does when afternoon turns into evening. The main part of the church was dome-shaped, with facets like those big multi-sided dice you use to play Dungeons & Dragons. Wings and additions were attached at angles. I didn't know what to expect as we pulled into the parking lot: scenes from "The Exorcist," a secret door leading to an underground laboratory, or a whole cult of brain-damaged beardos, all with matching powder-blue station wagons. I tried to keep my mind open.

Despite that, I was still surprised. The first thing we saw when we walked around to the church's back yard was a dozen dudes in armor, beating the hell out of each other with sticks. At first, all I could do was stare. They had shiny metal breastplates and knights' helmets that looked like they'd come from a museum. But they also wore huge hockey gloves with the makers' logos covered with gaffer tape. Their shields were painted with dragons and bears and medieval coats of arms, and had thick foam padding around the edges. They crashed into each other and I heard the heavy thud of wood against metal. They didn't use real swords, but instead swung thick wooden sticks at each other. That took away from the overall effect a little, but I'm sure it was a lot safer and it probably still hurt like hell.

With the mix of ancient and modern gear, they looked partly like medieval knights and partly like extras from a "Mad Max" movie. Mainly, though, they just looked damn neat. I've always appreciated big dramatic gestures, people doing goofy things in public because they feel like it. I suppose you don't last very long in drama club if you don't.

"Is this the place?" Macie whispered.

"I think it is." I took the card out of my pocket and looked at the swords-over-sun design on the back, then pointed to a long folding table, covered with a tan tablecloth, under a tree. The tablecloth had the same design sewn on it in red felt.

"Good evening! Welcome to the Shire of Three Rivers!" A woman in a long skirt and a top that I could only describe as "serving wench" came over from the table and smiled at us.

"Is this your first time here?" she asked.

Macie nodded and I said, "Yeah." After a second I realized that this probably wasn't enough, so I added, "Someone gave us this card. He was…"

I was about to describe him as a big guy with a beard, but now that the combatants had finished their battle and taken off their helmets, that description fit three-quarters of the males in the vicinity.

"Are you familiar with the SMRC?" asked the woman, who must have done this kind of thing before. When we responded in the negative, she continued. "Well, let me tell you a little bit about ourselves. We're the Society for Medieval Re-Creation. Some people call us the SMRC—" she pronounced it 'smirk' "—and our goal is to keep alive the customs, arts, crafts, and skills of the Middle Ages here in the modern world. The fun stuff, at least. We don't do a whole lot of plagues or inquisitions. We have a madrigal group, a bunch of us do calligraphy in some form or other, we have one of the most accomplished stained glass guilds in the whole kingdom, and, of course, there's the fighting."

One of the warriors walked past us, grim-faced, pale, and sweaty, on the way to the church's basement door. He had shaken off his hockey gloves and was cradling his right hand in the crook of his other arm.

"The fighters can get pretty serious. Here, let me give you some of our flyers."

She led us over to the table and was starting to load us up with literature when I saw someone I recognized.

"You made it!" It was the guy, the one who'd been following me around for so long. The one who had cast a magic spell on me yesterday. "I didn't know if you were going to be here or not."

"Hi, Cleve, this is Hal and Macie," the woman said. She had gotten our names while she was picking up the flyers for us.

Macie reached out to shake his hand, but instead of shaking, he kissed it and bowed low.

"Cleve of Arrowthorn, at your service, my lady." Then, to me, he said, "And well met, good sir. We are honored by your presence here today." My hand, fortunately, he shook.

"So, has Brocelinde been explaining the workings of our shire to you both?"

I nodded. Despite my history with this guy, I couldn't help smiling. I had heard of these SMRC people before, in a general way, the way one knows about the guys who dress up and re-enact Civil War battles, or people who wear furry animal costumes and go to conventions, but I had never seen them in the wild before. It may have been a trick of the light, which was making everything golden and hazy, but it seemed to me that everyone was having a good time here. There were other tables set up, with people giving demonstrations of needlework and carpentry. Someone in a red and green striped cap had started to play a wistful tune on a lute. Even the guy who had injured his hand was back again, with one hand swaddled in towels and ice packs, and the other holding a big brass goblet that he drank deeply from.

"I'll take it from here," Cleve said to Brocelinde and began to lead us off. As we moved away, I saw that Brocelinde had the same look my parents always had when my daredevil uncle John used to volunteer to take my cousins and me around the amusement park. I got the feeling she was afraid Cleve was going to toss us in with the stick-fighters and the rat-catcher general to see if we sank or swam.

As we walked, Cleve explained what was going on. "This is our quarterly demonstration day. It lets us show people what we're all about." He gestured over to where a small group of old ladies were gathered around two weavers in Viking dresses, working on a tapestry.

"You probably noticed the names already. A lot of us pick out medieval names to use while we're doing SMRC things. Here, I'm Cleve of Arrowthorn, Bailiff of the Shire of Three Rivers. At home, my name is Calvin, and I'm a regular guy." He noticed my expression and added, "More or less."

On the field of battle in front of us, a new set of fighters were tying on their helmets and tightening up their gloves.

"My lord Cleve! What say you?" one of them called.

"Pass!" Cleve, though I guess I should call him Calvin, flexed his elbow and grimaced. "Old war wound," he said to us. "We try to keep the fighting safe, but accidents do happen."

"Like in roller derby," Macie added.

"Exactly. A lot of strange things can happen in roller derby." He stared at us for a few seconds. A good long look, like he was trying to decide something about us.

"I imagine that's probably what you're here to talk about. Let's go inside," he said

The basement of the church was air conditioned, and far enough from the battle that we couldn't hear the crunch of wood on metal. A couple of civilians were watching an elderly man with thinning hair demonstrate calligraphy, and two others were sampling honey on thick slices of bread. It made me happy, for some foolish reason, to see that people had turned out for these demonstrations. Doing all this work for no response sounded awful.

Calvin led us onto the shallow stage at the other side of the basement, where a few chairs were scattered around. After pulling three of them into a triangle and making sure we were comfortable, he sat down.

He sighed, like someone gearing himself up to make a confession. "Where do I start?" he said to himself.

"How about with why you've been following me?" I asked.

"I'm going to have to go back a little further than that." He sat back in his chair and unlaced his tunic. Underneath was a t-shirt with the logo of a computer company that had gone out of business years ago.

"The SMRC began in 1969," he said. "It was founded by a group of people who believed there should be more romance in life, more honor, more adventure. In short, people who believed in magic."

Calvin paused for a second to watch some people enter the basement. "I won't bore you with the details, but it turned out they were right. As the founders of the society read more and more about what life was like in the Middle Ages, they ran across a number of old books that didn't get read a whole lot anymore. Most people thought they were just allegories, old folk tales, or private jokes by the authors, but some of the SMRC people took them seriously. Seriously enough to try out some of the formulas and incantations that they contained. And you know what? It worked."

Calvin had that intense look that people get when they're trying to convince you of something insane. In a chilling flash of insight, I realized that I must have had the same look when I showed Macie my picture of John Graze's gate.

"I'm sure this is hard to believe," Calvin said. "I didn't believe it either when I was your age. That's all right. Look around the room. Pick something."

I pointed to a book that sat on a display stand near the calligraphy guy. It had dark green leather covers and was tied closed with a black cord. There was a pattern on the leather that looked like Celtic animals chasing each other.

Calvin nodded and rubbed the tips of his fingers together, then mumbled something too low for me to hear. An instant later, Macie was holding the book in her hands. It didn't fly through the air. It simply appeared in a new place.

With a little noise of surprise, Macie let the book drop, and shoved herself backward so hard she almost fell out of her chair. I could understand her reaction. The sudden appearance of the book had been as unnerving as an awkward splice in a movie.

"Hey!" cried the calligraphy guy, who must have been the book's owner.

Calvin picked up the book and dusted it off. The calligraphy guy gave him a dirty look and went back to the manuscript page he was working on. No one else seemed to have noticed.

"So this is what the Society for Medieval Re-Creation is," Calvin said. "A lot of people who just enjoy playing knights and fair ladies, but also a few who really know how magic works."

"Magicians," I said.

"Wizards," Macie suggested.

"It's hard to pick a name, isn't it?" Calvin said. "We like to call ourselves Magi, but that sounds like a Christmas pageant to most people. To be honest, there's no name that makes everybody happy. But it's not too important. We know who we are and what we do."

"So what *do* you do?" I asked. If I had magical powers, I don't think I'd spend my time singing madrigals or playing the lute.

"We watch. We listen. We aren't the only ones who know how this power works, though we're some of the few who manage not to get corrupted by it." He handed the book to the calligraphy guy, who had stomped over to claim it. "It helps to have hobbies. And a circle of friends. It's going to sound melodramatic, but this stuff can separate you from the rest of the world pretty quickly, if you let it. Like it has with John Graze."

113

Calvin explained that he and the other SMRC magi had begun to develop inexplicable feelings of being watched, and several of them reported noises and shapes that had no natural source but refused to go away. To them, these were clear signs of another wizard exercising his powers. Then the shapes they saw from the corners of their eyes began to get clearer.

"His creatures," Calvin said. "Things he has raised up from nowhere and filled with life force from a dark magical place."

He paused and sighed. "I wish I could explain it better than this. Magic doesn't make sense. That makes it hard to talk about. If it made sense, we'd call it science or philosophy."

"It's okay. Go on," Macie said. She was hanging on his every word.

"We can see the creatures sometimes, but we can *sense* them more often than that. So we began to pay attention. After a while, I realized that I kept finding Hal near where the creatures had been, so we decided it would be a good idea to keep watch on him. We knew it couldn't have been you that summoned the things—"

I didn't know whether to be pleased or annoyed by that. Could they tell that I was a decent guy, or did they think I couldn't possibly have that much magical skill? Maybe both.

"—but we thought you might have been affected by them somehow. Marked. Cursed, so to speak."

"Cursed!" Macie said excitedly. She grabbed my arm and began to tell the story of the runes that John Graze had given her in the take-out menu. She talked amazingly fast, much faster than I'd ever heard her talk before. I hadn't expected her to believe Calvin's story—I certainly wasn't one hundred percent convinced—but she was completely won over. As she kept going, telling Calvin about Sandra's accident and transformation, and how Sandra didn't seem exactly like her sister anymore, I realized that she had been dying to talk to someone about this. It wasn't enough to talk to me, since I was as much in the dark as she was. But now, here was somebody who not only understood what she was talking about, but might even be able to give her some real answers, however bizarre those answers might turn out to be.

Calvin listened, nodding occasionally, while Macie talked. When she was done, the first thing he asked was, "You didn't happen to make a copy of those runes, did you?"

Macie shook her head.

"That would have been a pretty good idea," I said.

"Don't worry about it. If you'd tried, I think you would have been surprised by how hard it would have been. Your pen would have been out of ink, then you wouldn't have been able to find any paper, then there would have been a spider in your notebook and it would have bitten you and put you in a coma."

"Yikes."

"Curses aren't things to mess around with."

"It really was a curse?" Macie asked.

"You guys got it exactly right. Those runes, specially prepared, can be extremely dangerous. They act like a beacon, drawing his creatures toward whoever has them."

"But what about my sister?" Macie asked.

"I think one of the creatures saw an opportunity and took it," Calvin said. "When the victim is weak, they have their best chance to attack. So when it found someone who was already weak, and was already pretty close to you, it struck."

"And then did what?"

"It possessed her. It's trying to take her over from the inside. I don't know why the creatures are compelled to do this, but I'm sure John Graze does." Calvin cleaned his glasses with the hem of his tunic. "Either way, this is a pretty bad sign."

It seemed to me that we had seen nothing but bad signs ever since I made my first delivery to John Graze's house, so I asked Calvin why this was worse than anything else.

"Think of it this way: If he was really unhinged, I mean completely flipping insane, he probably would have done something like turn you into toads or have a giant bird carry you off. It's quick, it's permanent, and it's actually pretty darn easy to do. I'll show you." He motioned to the calligrapher. "Gary, come over here for a second."

"Absolutely not," was the response.

"Well, anyway, it's not a hard thing to learn. The fact that he hasn't done it means that he's not just lashing out. He has a plan."

"Why us?" Macie asked. "Why did he choose us to put this curse on?"

"I think I know why." I took a deep breath and started to describe what I had seen and heard yesterday, and what John Graze had told me. It was already hard to remember all the details. It felt like it had happened inside a nightmare, and it took a lot of concentration to still treat it like part of reality. When I had finished, Calvin sat back. He pushed his glasses up and massaged the bridge of his nose.

"I guess that explains why he'd come out of hiding to help direct a high school musical," Calvin said. "He's found a fuel source that he can use."

"Oh, boy," said Macie.

I had to admit, if John Graze was going to pick anywhere to feed on chaos and emotional instability, he'd made a pretty good choice. I wasn't even directly involved and I already knew about three breakups, one partner swap, and behavior from the "responsible adults" that would have put us all on "Dateline" if anyone ever found out.

"He's spreading chaos, strangeness," said Calvin. "He uses it to fray at the nature of our reality, and that paves the way for his creatures. The more creatures he can send out, the more people they can possess, and the more chaos they can create. It just feeds back on itself. Eventually he's going to have the power to do whatever he wants. Whatever that is."

"What should we do, then? We're the first ones he's targeted, right? We're the ones that have to do something, aren't we?" Macie asked.

She was right, of course. Even though there was a tiny part of myself that wanted Calvin to take over and wave us off, I knew I couldn't stay away. Since Macie wanted to help, too, I was doubly committed.

Calvin agreed with us. "Before we do anything, though, let me talk this over with the rest of my group. There are a few others in this chapter who study magic with me, and they might have some ideas, too."

"Are those the guys that jumped me?" I asked.

"They're very sorry about that."

Privately, I was wasn't too impressed to have those guys on our side, but maybe they might look better in a different situation.

"I won't lie to you," Calvin said, "this is the biggest thing any of us have ever faced."

"Great," I said.

"But it's why we're here. It's what we've studied and what we've devoted our lives to. You just gave us a lot of new information, so we're going to need to discuss what it all might mean. I'll get back to you as soon as we have an idea. Make sure you put your names and numbers on Brocelinde's sign-up sheet so we have a way to reach you."

Calvin called the next afternoon, and the three of us met at the Planet Caravan coffee house, just a couple of blocks from the Alhambra. It had textured, deep-yellow walls and artfully dilapidated furniture, but at the time I would have been perfectly happy trading aesthetics for a little distance and meeting at Starbucks by the mall. Calvin, however, was insistent.

"Here we can tap into the vibrations." He dunked a corner of his raspberry scone into his coffee. "I hate to say 'vibrations' because it makes me sound like a flake, but I can't think of a better word. You don't think I sound like a flake, do you?"

I shook my head, while nodding internally. We were sitting at a table in front of the bay window. Macie was drinking a latte and I was having an organic mint tea. Coffee never agreed with me.

"When we're close to a place where a sorcerer is operating, we can feel the energy in the air. We can get an idea of how ripe his plans are and how much time we've got left to react."

This made sense, but I couldn't help noticing how he'd also been wistfully eyeing the hot waitress with the nose ring, the batik skirt, the tube top, the belly chain, and the jangly ankle bracelets. Sometimes things can be the right choice for any number of reasons.

"So what do the vibrations tell you now?" Macie asked. This was the panic-infused last week before the show opened, and she'd been at rehearsals all day. There were hollows under her eyes and her expression was a bit feverish. I suspected it wouldn't be a good idea to push her too far. She still looked like a pixie, but a pixie who'd had enough for the day.

"Hmm…" Calvin ran a finger around the lip of his cup, then closed his eyes for a few seconds, as if tuning in to the local psychic aura. I couldn't tell if he was kidding or not. A few seconds later, he said, "I don't think there's a whole lot of time left. His creatures are appearing in the physical world. By itself, that's momentous. That's a very big step when it comes to this kind of work. Add that to the fact that this play he's working on is almost done, and you've got a whole lot of bad news."

"So what do we do?" I asked.

"We get into his house. Some time when he's not home, we get into his house and find clues about the nature of the magic he's practicing. Then we can find some way of undoing what he's done. Magic is very individualized. We need to understand his personal system if we're going to have a chance of stopping it.

"That's great. When do we go?" Macie sounded like she was ready to push away from the table and leave right now.

Calvin hesitated. "Your enthusiasm is… noble, but this is no job for you."

"And why not?" Macie asked, in the way that only someone who is short, female, and pugnacious can manage.

Calvin was groping for words, so I jumped in. "Macie, we actually do need you. We need you a lot. Think about it this way: What are we going to have to do? Get inside John Graze's house. And who is he? A famous recluse."

"He's only famous if you've memorized a bunch of old heavy metal records," Macie pointed out.

"But still a recluse, right? You'll give me that? When is the only time he's out of his house for sure? When he's at rehearsal. What's he going to think when, right in the middle of tech week, one of his leads disappears?"

"I'm not a lead, I'm supporting."

"Well, you're always a lead to me."

"Aww, that's sweet," said Calvin, which earned him an eye-roll from both of us.

"Either way, he's going to notice. If you're gone, he's going to say, 'Gosh, the girl who was the first victim of my world-destroying curse isn't here today. That seems suspicious, since she knows who I am and knows that I'm stuck here in rehearsals all day. Maybe I should unleash my army of invisible inhuman monsters right away, just to be sure.' "

She sighed and scowled at me, but it was more of a pout of defeat than a glare of anger. If Calvin hadn't been there, I would have kissed her.

Later, she and I were walking a couple of blocks over, through a row of old mansions that had recently been fixed up. I had some high-speed film in my Kodak Spectra 40 and wanted to try it out on the ivy-covered porticoes and decorative ironwork.

After a long period of silence, Macie said, "Be careful."

"I'm going to."

"I mean it. Don't do anything too risky."

"Are you sure you're okay with this?" I asked. "I mean, if you've got a serious problem with it…"

"What choice do I have? Do I like that you and Beardo are running the risks while I have to stand around and play decoy? No. But it's the only idea we've got. If this is going to help Sandra, then I'm all for it."

We had passed into some shadows, so I cranked open the aperture on my camera, then lifted it up to take her picture.

Macie turned away. "Cut it out," she said.

7

The next morning, Calvin met me at the McCullough branch library, which was on the east side of town and closer to John Graze's house. I left my car there and we took his small, dark blue Toyota.

"Excuse the mess," Calvin said as he lifted a pile of photocopied sheet music from the front seat and set it onto several other piles of stuff in the back. I saw magazines, old tattered manila folders, some carpentry books and even a wadded-up paper bag from Hardee's back there. There was a faint smell of mildew and the vinyl upholstery felt gritty. If this had been a friend's car—William's, for example—I wouldn't have thought twice about the mess, but Calvin was an adult. I had always assumed that you grew out of this kind of thing at some point.

"Do you think just the two of us are enough?" I asked as I lifted my camera strap out of the way and buckled myself into the passenger seat. I had kind of expected Calvin to bring the rest of the SMRC magicians as backup.

"Well, the other guys… They all had things to do."

"I see."

"I'll be honest," Calvin said. "I don't know how much help they would have been. I've been teaching a lot of those guys for a long time, but they haven't progressed as far as I'd like them to. It's easier for some people than it is for others."

We drove out to John Graze's neighborhood in Newburgh, then around the corner and down the side street to where Macie and I had gone when we spied on him the first time. Thinking about Macie made me nervous. I had no idea what might happen if we ran into a problem while searching the house. Would Calvin be able to protect us? Could he turn us invisible? Could he teleport us back home? I didn't ask him because I didn't want to know if the answer was "no." Instead, I watched as he carefully parked behind the run-down antique store, which still had the "closed" sign in the window, even though it was the middle of the morning. He took an army-green canvas bag from the trunk and we walked into the woods like we had every reason on earth to be there.

At the brick wall that surrounded John Graze's property, Calvin opened the bag and took something out. I had expected it to be some kind of mystical object—a magic mirror that let us see inside the house, or an ancient talisman that let us walk through walls. Instead, it looked like a thick package of metal bratwurst, bound up with plastic ties. Once Calvin snipped the ties with his multi-tool scissors, it became clear that this was a rolled-up flexible metal ladder with a hooked top. Calvin tossed the ends in the air a couple of times to test the weight, then heaved it over the edge of the wall, where the hooks bit in and held fast.

Calvin looked at me a little sheepishly. "I always wanted one of these. The guy who sold it to me is a friend of mine, so he gave me a good deal. Should I go first?"

Once on the other side of the wall, we crept the distance across the yard to the house. It couldn't have taken us more than a couple of minutes, but it felt like forever. It was hot as hell that morning, but it was overcast again and I was grateful for that. If we'd had to sneak around in bright daylight, I would have felt a lot more exposed.

Along the way, I saw that the stone idol in the back yard was gone. In its place, exactly where the idol had been, was an enormous, overgrown topiary bush. I pointed this out to Calvin, who nodded and said, "Different things look differently in the light of different fires." That did little to clear things up, and I didn't like the way it sounded.

We hid behind a stubby pine tree next to a window at the front corner of the house. Calvin reached up and gingerly pushed under the rail of the bottom panel. After a quick struggle, it slid a few inches upwards. Calvin raised his eyebrows at me. "Unlocked. Lucky us," he said.

He opened the window the rest of the way. "I guess this is it. Oh, wait…" He reached into his bag and held out something to me. It was a folded-up packet of paper, about as big as my thumb, bound with yellow thread and tied to a black cord long enough for me to wear around my neck.

"Put this on," he said. "I've got one, too. It should keep us safe from whatever's inside. *Safer*, anyway."

"What's in this?"

"Words. The right words, hopefully. And some other stuff. I can explain it more later, but right now just don't open it up, okay? And don't ever, ever eat it."

That sounded fair enough to me, so I put the thing around my neck and under my shirt, then followed Calvin through the open window.

The room we entered was almost bare of furniture, with only a couple of chairs and a coffee table, all of which looked like they were made to be appreciated rather than used. A few spotlights hung from tracks on the ceiling. If they had been on, they would have highlighted the pictures that hung on the walls in plain black frames. There weren't many of them, and they were spaced around the white walls like exhibits at a museum. Of course, I had to stop and look. Wouldn't you?

They were photos from his days in Left Hand Ritual. They were candid shots of the band rehearsing or getting ready to go on stage, or even performing. They were all black and white, and the photographer had done a good job. Left Hand Ritual were a lot heavier and more serious than most bands of that era, but it was still the Eighties, and even a normal-looking guy from back then can look odd to the eyes of someone from the future. These pictures, though, made the band look timeless. Looking at them, it was easy to forget about the bad albums and the ill-advised solo careers and all the other stuff that happens to rock stars. I found myself wanting to be those guys. To live the epic life that those pictures described under the light of my flashlight.

Then I got to a picture of John Graze by himself, on stage, smiling with grim satisfaction. He was looking directly at the camera, which gave his eyes the trick of following you around wherever you went in the room. That freaked me right out. A few seconds of staring at that picture and I was convinced that he *could* see us, that he could look into that room from wherever he was and see two idiots breaking into his house.

Calvin put a hand on my shoulder and nearly scared me to death. He pointed to the hall and made walking motions with his fingers. At another time, I would have found the fake commando-raid thing irritating, but right then I just nodded and followed along.

The dining room was as spotless and dust-free as the gallery had been. Again, everything was flat black against plain white walls. There was a long table with no tablecloth and six chairs around it, but no sign that anyone had used it recently.

"I bet this is just for company," I whispered to Calvin. Whispering felt like the right idea. "He probably eats somewhere else when he's by himself."

"Is he married?"

"He was. To one of the girls in Vixen. For a while. They broke up."

"Girlfriend?"

"Not that I know of."

"Let's find the TV, then," Calvin said. "We find the TV, we find where he lives."

As we made our way deeper into the house, it got darker. Outside, the clouds were much heavier than they had been. I wondered if the storm would hold off until we got out of here. We passed a few more rooms that all looked like they'd been styled for an interior decorator's magazine, then abandoned. Also, I didn't see anything else related to his music career. I hadn't thought his house would look like the inside of a Hard Rock Cafe, with guitars on the walls and spangly jumpsuits in display cases, but the man *had* been a legend. I'd expected something more than a few pictures.

The kitchen was pretty plain, too. Just a stove and a sink and some counters and cabinets. Calvin opened up the big stainless steel fridge and stood there for a second enveloped in the light.

"Come look at this," he said softly.

The fridge was empty. No fruit, no vegetables, no leftover pizza or Korean takeout containers. No carton of milk or six-pack of beer. It didn't even look used.

"There's nothing there," I said.

"Nearly." Calvin crouched down with a grunt and picked up something that lay in the corner of the bottom shelf. It was a glass soda bottle, crusted with a cold film of dirt and stopped with a stained cork.

Calvin rubbed at the label and let the dirt fall onto the spotless black-and-white tile. He stood up and showed it to me.

"Double Cola. They used to have this all over the place when I was a kid."

He held the bottle up to the refrigerator light and tilted it back and forth. A red-brown liquid sloshed around inside the bottle. It was about three-quarters full. It could have been some sort of special formulation of designer root beer, but I'm pretty certain it wasn't.

"This could be important." Calvin wrapped the edge of his t-shirt around the cork for a better grip, then pulled it out. Very carefully, he poured a few drops into the palm of his hand. He stared at them for a few seconds, then licked them. He rolled his tongue around in his mouth, which made him look like a wine taster. However, there probably aren't very many wine tasters who go to work in black t-shirts with the Green Lantern logo on them. He put away the bottle and stood still for a second while I waited for him to talk about its "earthy hues" or "cinnamon notes" or whatever. Instead, he launched himself toward the sink and retched his guts out.

I stood around pretending not to notice, the way you do when someone nearby is doing something disgusting. When it seemed like he was done, I asked, "Are you okay?"

"Yeah. No problem."

"You sure about that?"

"Really, I'm fine." He drank a handful of water from the sink. "I expected that."

"It wasn't blood, was it?"

Calvin shook his head. "Blood? Oh, no. If it was blood, that would have been great."

"Really?" That was an odd usage of 'great,' I thought.

"If he was drinking blood, then we'd know what he was and how to deal with him. Actually, depending on the blood, I could have probably figured out what his next move was, too."

"You can tell blood apart by taste?"

"I think the TV's over here," Calvin said, and led us out of the kitchen.

He was right. The next room over was a luxurious living room with leather couches (black, of course) and a huge TV dominating one wall.

"I don't think he does much living here," I said. This room was as spotless and sterile as all the other rooms we'd seen. I pointed to the couches and their perfectly formed cushions, without a single butt-print anywhere. "Look at this. These haven't even been touched."

Calvin wasn't paying attention. He was peering at a silver all-in-one computer that sat on a minimalist black wire table along the wall. We fired it up and it was, of course, protected by a password. While Calvin ran through all the magic words he thought a warlock might use to secure his MP3 files and porn collection, I checked the window. It had started to rain. After a few minutes Calvin gave up on the computer and we continued our tour.

That's when things got weird.

We opened the door that led to the room behind the kitchen, then froze, too shocked to go any farther.

"Well," said Calvin. "I think this is what we're looking for."

Have you ever seen one of those documentary shows that feature some poor slob who's lost the ability to throw anything out and instead just piles up random crap in their house until they have to dig tunnels to get from room to room? This little room at the back of John Graze's house was just like that. Except it was worse, because you could tell it wasn't the result of someone's mental illness. This was much scarier, because it had been done deliberately. How did I know? It's the same way an abstract painting looks different than somebody throwing paint randomly at a canvas: you could see the intelligence behind it, even if you didn't understand the reasoning.

A short tower of cardboard boxes, with fist-sized holes punched in them, held netted bags full of rotting vegetables. A naked, red-headed mannequin had been mutilated with a reciprocating saw. Men's clothes, caked with tar and sparkling with metallic filings, were folded neatly and stacked in a corner. Lines of chalk dust criss-crossed the matted carpet. They snaked around and under the other piles of debris, like a road map buried on the floorboards of a filthy car.

Then there was the writing on the walls. Every-where we looked, every inch of the walls was covered with diagrams, formulae, strings of gibberish words and numbers that ran in circles, backwards, upside-down and on top of each other. Parts of the writing had been done with a brush, but other sections looked like they'd been put on with fingers. It was all in a dull red that I hoped was paint. Some of the diagrams I recognized from different Left Hand Ritual album covers and liner notes.

Every so often there were English bits I could read, like "The mouth that eats itself" or "Master of the Spheres, reveal thyself in ecstasies of pain and joy. Draw forth your life from the wrack of the soul." It was just enough to make me glad I couldn't read the rest.

"This is his system. This whole room is the expression of his magical system," Calvin said. I couldn't help noticing that he sounded a whole lot less confident than I wanted him to. He sounded like an exterminator who'd been called out to deal with a wasps' nest in a tool shed, only to find that the shed was inhabited by two-headed mutant flesh-eating wasps from Dimension X.

"It's amazing. We have to record this. Take some pictures," he said, then noticed the camera I'd been carrying around.

"What is that?"

"It's a Kodak Signet 40. I just found it last month. It's awesome."

"Is it digital?"

"Are you kidding?"

"Do you know how to use it?"

I'm always amazed that, when you show most people a camera with no electronics, they assume it's as hard to operate as the Hubble Telescope. "Sure. You turn a dial, you press a button. Easy peasy." To be honest, I wouldn't have minded a big digital camera with its ugly, idiot-proof flash right about now, or even the camera in my phone under the front seat of Calvin's car, but it was too late to admit that.

The rain was lashing at the windows now. I could see little whitecaps forming on the pool in John Graze's back yard. It was pretty dark in here. Light enough to see easily, but the eye could work a lot harder to make things out than a camera could. After a quick discussion we flipped on the lights, which made the room even more disgusting. A lot of the really gross stuff had been hidden by the gloom. My eyes drifted over to something in the corner, and before I could look away I realized that a lot of those stories about Left Hand Ritual in the Eighties might have been true after all.

"Get as much of the walls as you can," Calvin told me. I opened the aperture as far as it would go and braced my elbows against my chest, in order to have the best chance of taking clear pictures.

"I had hoped to find his notes, or an altar, something with a recognizable style so I could figure out how he does his workings," Calvin said. He poked around in the piles of garbage while I kept taking pictures. "I think this whole room is his notes. We're seeing it from the inside, which is why it doesn't make sense to us. I hope that's what it means, anyway."

He paused. "Do you feel that?"

"Feel what?"

"I don't know how to describe it. The air is wrong. You live with magic for a long time and you start to get used to how it feels. Your senses change. Some open up, some fade. You get new ones entirely, sometimes. But you get used to the way it's supposed to feel. Things don't feel that way here."

I shuffled around and tried to find a good angle for some wide shots. "I think even a normal person could tell you something's not right here."

"It's worse than that. It's like, say, you've got perfect pitch. Somebody deliberately plays a bunch of bad notes. De-tunes his violin strings and just saws away on it. You're going to really feel that. That's what it's like in here. Wait— Come look at this."

Calvin had found something behind a waist-high rampart of wet things in garbage bags. At first, it didn't look like much, just a tangle of old blankets and towels. Then I saw that they'd been tangled in a very particular way, to form an oval shape with a depression in the center.

"It's his bed," I said.

"His nest," Calvin corrected.

It smelled like wet rust and the nauseating sweetness of rotting food. Calvin tiptoed around to get a better look. It wasn't easy. The pathways around the room weren't meant for someone his size.

I shook my head. "He always seemed so... clean."

"We see what we're supposed to see, sometimes."

A sharp crack of thunder sounded somewhere nearby.

Calvin knelt down and poked cautiously at the bedding. Credit where it's due: I would never have done that in a million billion years.

Scattered through the bedding were little strange things—metal from beer cans chopped up to make tiny figurines, stones and feathers tied together, stuff like that. Calvin held one up to the light and scowled at it. He was about to say something when the light flickered wildly for an instant. An enormous clap of thunder rattled the house so severely that I thought someone was shaking the windows, trying to get in.

I got off one more picture before the lights went out completely. "We'd better go," Calvin said.

"Why? Do you feel something?"

Calvin pointed to his wristwatch. "It's just about three-thirty. That's when the rehearsal ends. We want to get out of here before he gets back."

We retraced our steps out of the house and sprinted through the rain to reach the wall at the edge of his property. I ran with my camera tucked under my shirt. For all the virtues these old cameras have—good lenses, great design, no batteries—I'm pretty sure they're not very water-resistant. We scaled Calvin's metal ladder again and in a few minutes we were driving away in his Toyota, dripping on the seats.

I was surprised to notice I was feeling guilty. Sure, we'd just broken the law, but that wasn't it. What I felt bad about was invading his privacy. It doesn't make much sense, but it was true. Calvin and I had just poked around in some place that John Graze had never shown to any other person on earth. It felt like reading someone's diary, seeing that part of them that they never show to anyone else. I knew it was ridiculous to feel that way, but I couldn't shake it.

"Have you ever seen anything like that?" I asked as we crawled through the thunderstorm back to town.

"Like that? Sure. All the time."

"Really?"

"No. Not at all. I don't even know what half of those things were supposed to mean. I was just saying that to make you feel better."

"It didn't work. So what do we do now?"

"I get together with the rest of the magi in the SMRC and tell them about the parts I did recognize, and we wait for you to get that film developed."

"I'll do it tonight."

"You know how to develop film?"

"Sure I do. Besides, even if I didn't, you don't think it would be a good idea to drop this off at Walgreens, do you?"

"You're absolutely right. Especially the Walgreens on Heidelbach Avenue. That place is filled with evil vibrations. Who knows what they've got chained up in the back room there."

I hoped he was kidding, but didn't want to ask and be told no, so I reached over and turned on the radio. It came up with a grinding metallic shriek and my heart did a flip-flop. Fortunately, it turned out to be the tail end of an emergency weather alert, instead of the latest manifestation of John Graze's curse.

"Once again, there is a severe thunderstorm warning for Pike, Posey, Gibson, and Vanderburgh counties," said the disembodied mechanical voice that always made any emergency weather announcement twice as scary. The voice went on to say that strong winds, damaging hail, and lightning strikes had been reported and anyone in the listed counties should seek shelter immediately.

Calvin smirked and put in a Hüsker Dü CD to shut up the robot weatherman. I understood his point. After what we'd just seen, it seemed kind of ridiculous to be afraid of a little weather. This attitude, which made us either heroes or idiots, seemed perfectly natural. But it turned out that this wasn't what Calvin meant at all.

He muttered a string of strange words, then touched the windshield with two fingers. I felt a momentary lurch, as if I were in an elevator that had shot upward, then it was much easier to see out.

"That's better," Calvin said. The rain wasn't even hitting the car anymore. About an inch before it reached us, it simply disappeared, vanished into thin air. Instead of driving through a blinding downpour, it looked to us like we were going through a mild fog.

"Nobody should notice anything unless they look closely, but I'll keep the wipers on for effect." Calvin sounded extremely pleased with himself.

"Wow," was all I could say.

138

"We're not supposed to make ourselves conspicuous, but I think this is acceptable." As I continued to stare dumbfounded out the window, Calvin went on. "This is magic, Hal. It's power. Real power. Mastery of reality. That's why we can't let this John Graze character keep doing what he's doing. I recognized a few of the formulas back there, and they're the starting points for things that make the curse he gave you and your girlfriend look like a mild cold."

"And you have enough... *magic* to stop him?" It still felt ridiculous to say this kind of stuff out loud.

Calvin nodded. "I think so. If we don't, it'll be the end of the world." A perfectly timed bolt of lightning lit up the sky all around us.

"Sorry. That was me," Calvin said. "I couldn't help it."

"I don't mean to be rude, but you've got a weird sense of humor."

"Comes with the territory, I'm afraid. When this is all over, I can teach you a little bit about magic if you want. It's a lot like bee keeping or snake charming: it's less scary once you know something about it."

When we got back to the library, he got out with me and stood in the rain with his hands on the hood of my car while he said a few more words under his breath.

"This'll get you home safe," he explained.

"Safe from the storm, or safe from... him?"

"Definitely the first. Probably not the second."

On the way home, I had to detour around a couple of downed limbs and flooded intersections, but I made it back in one piece. The house was dark. The power was out, which meant I couldn't develop my film right away. I probably could have done it all by touch in the dark, but these photos were a little more important than the stuff I usually developed. I decided to wait.

I slept surprisingly well that night, considering everything I'd seen the day before. No nightmares, no visions of long-jawed, red-eyed things crouching at the foot of my bed, just the occasional return to semiconsciousness as a big bolt of lightning lit up the outdoors and rattled the windows. When I woke up for good, the first thing I did was to rush down to the little curtained-off area of the basement that I use as a darkroom. A while later, I hung up my negatives and went upstairs for breakfast. Dad had the TV on, which was rare. Neither of us really like to have the rest of the world yelling at us until we've been awake for a couple of hours.

The TV was turned to Action 14 News. They were talking about the chain of storms that had rolled through the area, one after another, last night. The weatherman, normally jolly, had shifted gears into his serious mode. He was describing the path of the storm, and how it had been one of the strongest things to hit the area in decades. From time to time he would introduce various members of the Action 14 News Team who were out at the scenes of storm-related damage.

Apparently, the large number of lightning strikes had caused a few fires, even in the middle of the pouring rain. I froze mid-toast-bite when I saw where one of the reporters was standing: St. Mark's Methodist Church. Fire hoses snaked through the lower windows and into the basement. Firemen in their black and yellow raincoats ran back and forth in the background as they tried to make sure the fire was out.

I stared at the TV. St. Mark's. Home of the Lamasco chapter of the SMRC. The SMRC, home of Calvin and the rest of his wizards. Was it a coincidence?

"That was some storm last night," Dad said.

"Yeah. Hey, I've got to go do some things this morning before I go to work. See you later, okay?"

As I drove into town, I rolled down the window and took a big breath of the sweet, post-thunderstorm air. I dug into my stack of old cassette dubs in the little compartment between the front seats. I put one in and pressed play. Left Hand Ritual. Shuddering, I yanked the tape out and threw it in the back seat. When I realized what I'd just done, I felt a little melancholy. My favorite band, the one I always listened to when I needed some encouragement or escape, now made my skin crawl. That didn't seem fair.

At St. Mark's, the excitement was almost over. There was one fire truck left, and they were coiling their hoses in preparation for leaving. The news van must have been long gone by this point. I got out and looked around. The main doors were open and a couple of the basement windows were broken. There were puddles of water everywhere, but after the storm that was true of the whole city.

"It could have been a lot worse." One of the firemen, mistaking me for a distraught parishioner, had walked over while I wasn't paying attention.

"What happened?"

"Damnedest thing. Lightning. As far as we can tell, it hit the lightning rod up top, ran down the side, and something jumped it over to the drywall in the basement. It started burning from there. Burned out a couple of rooms, but it didn't get any of the supporting stuff. You guys ought to be able to start up again in a week or two."

"Great," I said, half-dazed.

"It's pretty rare that you see lightning start a fire from the bottom up, but that's what we've got here. It usually happens with old barns, things with lightning rods that have never been checked in a hundred years. Weird." The fireman shook his head, which sent little droplets of water spraying all over the place. "This whole storm was weird. Somebody told me there was an apartment building downtown that had one single room burned out by lightning. Just one room. Crazy. You want to know the truth?"

I nodded, even though I thought I might already know the truth.

"Nobody knows how lightning works, or why it does what it does," he said. "Just one of those things." He glanced up at the untouched cross atop the geodesic church building and went back to coiling his hoses.

If my suspicion was right, and John Graze's magic had caused this fire, then there was a pretty good chance that he'd done it as revenge for invading his house. I needed to get in touch with Calvin so we could figure out what to do next. I drifted over to a green car in the parking lot. It had SMRC coat-of-arms stickers on the back window and a bumper sticker that read, "My other car is a trebuchet." Whoever owned this car, I was sure they'd know where I could find Calvin. A minute later, a side door in the church opened and woman in a long patchwork skirt tottered out. She was the one who had handed us the flyers at the SMRC meeting. After a second's thought, I remembered that her SMRC name was Brocelinde. She looked dazed and sickened, like someone who had just seen where hot dogs came from.

"Hi," I said. "Is everything all right?"

She shook her head and held up what must have been, before the fire, a large, elaborate, leather-covered book. Now it was sort of a book rind, just a spine and a few charred scraps attached to it.

"All of them are like this. Everything we had here. All our history for the past thirty years. It's all burned," she said. "All gone. I can't believe it."

"I'm sorry." It wasn't enough, but what else can you say?

Brocelinde sighed the deepest sigh I've ever heard, then said, "At least no one was hurt. That's something."

"Yeah," I said. "I hate to bother you right now, but do you know where I can find Calvin?"

"Calvin?"

"Oh, right. He has another name here, doesn't he?" I could see where the whole medieval-persona idea would be fun, but it had to be confusing as hell. Even with just one name, I could hardly keep track of my own life, and I had a life that was hardly more complicated than a zoo animal's. Fortunately, she was able to figure out who I meant pretty quickly. She rattled off Calvin's phone number, which I wrote down on my hand. I thanked her, made a few more sympathetic noises, then drove off to my job while she went back to sifting through the ashes.

8

When I got to work, I used Calvin's number to find his address in the reverse lookup, but I had to wait until Jaya's back was turned. I love my aunt—she's a great cook and a fairly tolerable boss, but she's not the type of person who takes "nothin' " as an acceptable answer for "What are you doing?"

According to the lookup, Calvin lived on the second block of Mulberry Street. I'd built up a pretty good map of the city in my head by this point, and I was sure that his address was one of those big old Victorian houses that were two streets away from the river. Well, before the 1937 flood they were two streets away from the river. Now they were two streets away from the levee. Not as nice a view, but less chance of floating down the Ohio River every spring. Fair exchange, I thought. Anyway, the address was a short drive from the restaurant. It was also just a few blocks away from the Alhambra Theater, which made me nervous.

I did some prep work for Jaya until Nate got there. Once the door opened, I waited tables for the handful of regulars who couldn't get to noon without a kimchee fix. The delivery calls started earlier than usual that day. There were a lot more of them, too. Everybody was busy cleaning up from the storm, it seemed, and nobody felt like cooking. Everybody felt like tipping big, though, which I appreciated. I wondered if they were grateful to have one less thing to deal with. No one from Calvin's neighborhood called in an order that day, so I didn't have a chance to find out exactly where he lived until I got off work later that afternoon.

His address was right where I thought it was, on the short side of the block, in the middle of a row of houses all more than a hundred years old. They had ornamental iron railings along the balconies, and one had a square cupola with a weather vane at the top. Tall trees with overhanging limbs shaded the houses and put the street into deep shadow. Calvin's address was a stocky, two-story house with a slate roof. There were four mailboxes on the columned porch, so the place must have been cut up into apartments. As I pulled up to it, I began to feel sick. One of the bay windows in the top floor had been broken, and the frame was singed black all around. I remembered the story the fireman had told me this morning: another fire caused by mysterious lightning, which had burned out just one single apartment.

I got out of the car in a daze and stood at the foot of the porch steps. The boarded-up window seemed like an eyepatch over a gouged-out eye. I tried not to look at it. This couldn't be a coincidence. As I stood there staring, the front door opened and a girl stepped out. She was a few years older than me, about the age of Macie's sister Sandra, with long blonde hair and round sunglasses. She wore purple running shorts and a white tank top. She was really good-looking, but what I noticed first was her camera. She had a vintage black Rolleiflex slung around her neck. It was a twin-lens camera, the kind you hold at waist level and sight through a periscope-like reflector on the top. I've always wanted one, but I could never pay the internet auction prices, and I've never found one at a garage sale.

"Nice camera," I said. I wished I hadn't left my own camera in the car. I could have proved to her that I was a fellow camera person.

"Thanks. I just got it. I love old cameras."

"Me too," I said.

She smiled at me. I tried to see her eyes through the sunglasses, but the lenses were super dark.

"Do you know what happened there?" I pointed up to the burned window.

"Lightning. It was during the storm last night."

I looked around. There were a few small limbs down, but not an exceptional amount of damage. The whole street was still canopied by tall trees. If lightning

147

had hit that window, it would have had to go through the layer of trees first.

"I actually slept through it," she continued. "I didn't know anything about it until I heard the fire trucks."

"And it just got that one room?"

She nodded. "I talked to one of the firemen later, and he said he'd never seen anything like it. That apartment was burned to a crisp, but everything on the other side of the wall wasn't even touched. As far as he could tell, the whole house should have burned down. That's when his partner told him to shut up."

"What about the guy who lived there?"

"Calvin? I don't know. I mean, I haven't seen him, but I didn't see an ambulance or anything, either. Maybe he wasn't there."

"So you haven't seen him at all today?"

"Nope." She shook her head. "If that happened to me, I don't know what I'd do. I think we're all going to have to move out until they fix everything up again. It's a shame. I like this place. But it's probably a good idea. Do you mind if I take your picture?"

I tried to look interesting for one two-hundredth of a second, then drove away. I didn't know how I felt. Obviously, none of this was random. That fact couldn't have been clearer if another bolt of lightning had scored "Stay the hell out of my house. Sincerely, John Graze" on the hood of my car. But there was still so much I didn't know. For example, where was Calvin?

I refused to believe that Calvin, who had been skillful enough to push the raindrops out of our way yesterday, had been caught by surprise and incinerated inside his apartment. He must be hiding somewhere, I thought. I had to find him, or some of his SMRC people, and hand over the pictures I'd taken inside Graze Manor. With luck, that would give them enough information to figure out what to do next. I hoped it would. All I knew for sure was that right now it was time to pick up Macie.

By the time I got to the civic center parking lot, the fluffy white clouds had congested into a solid dark mass. I had passed at least a dozen people cleaning up storm damage on the way over here, and as I walked to the entrance I suspected they were going to have to do it all over again. All of a sudden, I felt like the approaching storm was looking for me personally, that it was coming back to finish the job it had started with St. Mark's and Calvin's apartment. I hurried inside.

I stayed in the steel and glass lobby of the civic center, and didn't sneak in to watch the end of the rehearsals. I didn't want to run the risk of encountering John Graze, so I stayed within convenient fleeing distance of an exit. Twenty minutes later, a number of kids with notebooks and scripts in their hands began to trickle out of the auditorium. I recognized a few of them, including William and a couple of others from the drama club at

North. I said hello and talked a little while, but most of them were interested in getting out of there to finish scrubbing off the dress-rehearsal makeup and enjoy what time they had left until the opening.

I watched them go. They were all carrying the same kind of notebook: thick and black, with leather covers, the kind you find in art supply stores but usually put down because it's too expensive. Some of the cast were leafing through them, and I saw that the pages were all blank. Then Macie came out, laughing at something Micah Tomey had just said to her. They were both carrying notebooks, too.

"Hi, Hal," she said.

It seemed to me that they had taken a half step away from each other when they saw me, but I couldn't be sure.

"What's that?" I pointed to their books.

"John gave these to us," Micah said. "Right before we were about to go, he stood up and gave this little speech about how much of an honor it had been to help us with the show, how it had re-ignited his own enthusiasm for music. Then he handed these out to everybody. He said he wanted to give us something to remember this time with. He told us to write down as much as we could remember about the rehearsal and the performances."

Micah flipped through the pages. "It's a nice book. I honestly didn't think he liked us that much." Impulsively, he held it out to Macie. "Sign mine, will you?"

Macie opened the book. Down the inside front cover was a column of black runes, just like the ones John Graze given her. Even the brushwork lettering was the same.

Macie and I shared a quick glance. I could see from her expression that she had something more to tell me.

Micah didn't say anything about the runes, but kept talking as Macie signed. "Didn't he used to be in a band or something? Somebody told me it was some hair band. Can you imagine?"

"Thanks," he said once she was finished. "Here, let me do yours." He wrote a suspiciously long inscription, then gave the book back. "See you tomorrow, all right?" Micah put his hand on her arm for a second, grinned, then jogged out to catch up with a couple of friends from the chorus.

Macie and I drifted away from the auditorium doors to where we could talk privately.

"They can't see it," I said.

Macie nodded. "None of them can see it. Every book I looked in has those runes, but I'm the only one who can see it. You and me, I mean."

"His magic is getting better."

"Look at this." She opened her book. It didn't have runes on the inside cover, but instead there was a message:

Macie, I have enjoyed working with you very much. Much more than the others, for reasons I suspect you know. Break a leg, and give my regards to Hal as well. He certainly deserves them.

All the best,

John Graze

"No one else can see this," Macie said. "I asked. To them, it's just a blank page. Like theirs."

We cleared out of the civic center and I drove Macie home. I took the long way, driving north on Stringtown Road. It took more time, but there wasn't as much traffic so it was easier to talk.

"Mr. Graze is using those runes to draw his creature-things toward everyone in the cast," Macie said. "We've got to let Calvin know what's happening."

I opened my mouth, then closed it again. What should I tell her about Calvin? What did I know for sure? For all I knew, he was perfectly fine, despite his apartment burning down. Macie already looked worried, so maybe I should keep my suspicions to myself until I had proof.

"What do you think he's going to do next?" she asked.

"Whatever it is, I bet he'll wait until the show is over." When I saw her puzzled expression, I added, "For some reason, John Graze is invested in this show. That's what you've been telling me, right?"

She shrugged. "I guess. He really does seem to care that we do a good job. A lot of the time, he acts like he cares more than Mr. Fanshaw."

"This show is like his, I don't know, fantasy football team or something. He wants it to do well." I hesitated for a second while trying to find the right word. Having talked to John Graze in the Alhambra, and poked around inside his nest, I thought I had some idea of how his mind worked. "He wants to demonstrate that he can be successful at whatever he tries. That's the kind of person he is."

"I could believe that," Macie said. "Do you really think Calvin can take care of him?"

"Absolutely. John Graze is just some bored heavy metal guy who wants his audience back. Calvin is a professional."

"Yeah. You're right."

I turned left at the country club and headed for Macie's house. I totally should have tried out for the summer musical. I'm a great actor.

It was raining again by the time we got to her house. Not a big, frightening twilight-of-the-gods storm like yesterday, but just a regular storm. We ran inside and Macie gave me a quick kiss before running upstairs to get ready. We had made plans to see a movie tonight to take Macie's mind off of the next day's opening. She's not the kind of person who normally has a problem with stage fright, but when you're playing a singing, dancing, bisexual performance artist in front of everyone you know, including your elderly, deeply Romanian Orthodox grandparents, things can get a little nerve-wracking. I was glad for the distraction, too. Maybe she wouldn't badger me to call Calvin right away, and I could put off admitting I didn't know where he was.

I was about to get comfortable on the couch and wait when I realized I wasn't the only person in the living room. Macie's sister Sandra had been sitting in one of the armchairs, still as a statue.

"Hi, Hal," she said.

Startled, I babbled something stupid and sat down on the couch, as far away as I could get without ending up in the kitchen. Even before her concussion and subsequent possession, I was never quite comfortable around Sandra. She had that kind of aura that a lot of roller derby girls had, the sense that she could snap you off at the knees if she felt like it, and she knew it and she knew you knew it. Now, of course, there was something else as well.

"How's the play coming?" Sandra asked.

"Okay, I think. Macie's the best one there. You know, obviously."

"I don't understand how you guys do it. I think I would honestly die if I had to sing in front of people. I can hardly bear to watch when Macie does it."

"After a while you don't even think about it. You just jump in there."

Despite the harmless nature of the conversation, I would have leaped off the sofa and hidden under the hall table if any opportunity had presented itself. I felt like I was talking to someone on a really bad mobile phone connection. Sandra's responses were a split second off from being normal, just off enough to be noticed. The same with her voice. The pitch or the timbre was wrong somehow in a way that I couldn't describe, only feel. The fact that she was sitting in front of the picture window, with lightning going off behind her, didn't help either.

The lights flickered for a second, then went back to normal.

"I hope that doesn't kill Dad's computer," Sandra said. "I think he left it on."

"Is lightning a problem here?" I asked this just to be making conversation. Where I lived, out where it was still more rural, we tended to lose appliances to storms like they were sacrifices to some temperamental weather god.

"Not too much," she said. "It's just that Dad got a new computer and he's—"

There was a viscera-rattling wave of thunder, and the lights went out.

"Oh, great. Hal, do you think you could reach around the corner and grab the flashlight?"

I didn't say anything. After the power had gone out, the lightning had kept flashing, and for an instant I got a look at Sandra illuminated by the storm.

It wasn't Sandra.

It was one of those eggplant-skinned creatures. Its mouth hung open in a tooth-filled circle. Its eyes, perfectly visible in the darkness, stared right at me.

The worst part was that I could see the creature and still hear Sandra talking to me. I felt like I was in two places at once and slowly asphyxiating in both of them. I was paralyzed by the conviction that if I moved a muscle, the thing would leap on top of me and gnaw into my chest.

Then the lights came on and everything was back to normal. Sandra was there, I was there. Most importantly, oxygen was there and I took a huge thankful gulp of it.

"I'm going to go see," Sandra said. I wasn't sure what she was going to go see, or even how long she'd been talking, but I nodded pleasantly as she went into the kitchen. A second later, I heard footsteps on the staircase and was pleased that it was Macie and not some fresh wave of ghouls.

"Ready to go?" she asked, right before I grabbed her and pushed her back against the doorframe, kissing her as hard as I'd ever done. I was already kissing her before my mind even decided to do it. Maybe it was because she looks so damn perfect without her makeup, like a beautifully art-directed ad for a line of "natural" cosmetics. Or maybe I didn't want her to see how freaked out I was. Both were possible.

"You okay there?" she asked, nudging me back a little. "Come on, let's go see the movie."

I began to feel increasingly guilty as we drove to the theater. I knew I should tell her about Calvin, but I couldn't quite do it. She had enough to deal with right now. I'd tell her when the show was done. I hated keeping things from her, but I told myself that it wouldn't be for long. Just a couple of days.

9

The next evening I watched the opening night of the Vanderburgh County School System's all-city summer musical. I thought they did a fine job, but it was a little hard to sit through. First of all, it's always tough to watch your friends sing or dance or do whatever on stage in front of hundreds of people. It's impossible to just sit back and enjoy the show, because you worry about whether things are going all right, and you feel like you have to keep sending psychic vibrations of goodwill their way just so they don't fall to pieces.

On top of that, there was a part of me that wanted to be up there, too. Despite what I had told myself, I loved performing. I loved being on stage in whatever part I could get. I didn't realize how strong this feeling was until I wasn't doing it.

Also, I was full of concern about evil wizards and phantom monsters. I was often so busy scanning the cast members' faces for any signs of incipient demonic possession that I forgot to pay attention to the show. By the end, when everyone who was supposed to have died had done so, and everyone who survived had sung about it, I was exhausted.

After the show, most of the cast and crew ended up at the Mongol Dream Barbecue Restaurant on Diamond Avenue. They picked it not because anyone was much of a fan of Mongolian barbecue, but because it was located in a building that used to be a Burger Barn years ago, and still had the distinctive barn architecture, complete with silo and windmill. The food wasn't bad at all, but the chance to be part of some alternate-universe Mongolian hoedown was the real attraction.

I kept an eye out for any signs of strange behavior among the rest of the cast, but I didn't see anything out of the ordinary. Relatively speaking, I mean. It *was* a bunch of teenage actors who had just gotten off stage, drunk on applause, adrenaline, and themselves. Most of them, talking at the top of their lungs, were still performing. If I'd been an outside observer, I would have wanted to throw a bucket of water on us, I'm sure.

Macie and I were working through a tall plate of spicy shaved beef and rice. When no one was paying attention, we exchanged conspiratorial glances.

"Has anything new happened?" I whispered.

She shook her head. "Not that I've heard. I asked a few more people if they noticed anything odd about their books, but they acted like I was nuts, so I quit."

"Did you see John Graze there tonight?"

"No. Was he out in the audience?"

"I don't know."

"This waiting is driving me crazy. Have you heard anything from Calvin—"

At that point, Macie was dragged off by Micah Tomey to get her to sing a song from *Kiss Me, Kate*, which they had both been in last year. I couldn't help noticing that he sang with his arm around her waist, the same way I couldn't help noticing that one of the big barbecue-slicing knives on the side of the central cooker would be just perfect for stabbing someone. I rubbed my eyes to erase the vision. I'm usually not that violent, not even in daydreams, and it surprised me how much I wanted to pick the knife up and see what it felt like to shove it between his ribs. I told myself to put it out of my mind, that I was just overwrought. After all, Macie and I had been dating other people when we first hooked up, which happened to be during the run of a play, so I was bound to get a little upset when I saw something that reminded me of that same situation. I told myself to go back to my barbecue. And think up a reason not to go to these parties in the future.

Over the next few days, while the musical went on, I tried to keep myself busy. I worked. I delivered chajangmyun and shrimp fried rice. I bussed tables. I listened to Nate, the lumbering, burly line cook, complain about life as a graduate student. I even filled in for him on a couple of shifts until I burned my hand on the range and Jaya got nervous about the insurance. I made prints of all the pictures I had taken in John Graze's house. Much to my surprise, just about everything turned out. It all looked so different in black and white. The pictures felt like they were from a film set or an art installation, rather than a real-life place. There was a barrier between the photographs and the reality of what Calvin and I had seen. Normally I'd say that good pictures wouldn't put up a barrier like that, but this time I was grateful to have it. The memory of the thing was bad enough—all I wanted was a record of what I had seen, not a way to transport me back.

I couldn't make sense of what I saw in the pictures, no matter how hard I tried. All I had to help me with this were *The Magicians Speak*, a few other library books, and junk off the internet, but none of it could give me any insight. Nothing made any sense. It wasn't like Calculus or Korean, either, which didn't make sense but looked like they *would* if I tried harder. This felt like it was from another planet. I carried the pictures around in a folder in my car, just in case I ran into Calvin again. I wasn't having any luck finding him any other way.

As far as Macie knew, though, Calvin and his assistants were studying the photos diligently, and were only days away from defeating John Graze's plans. I felt like a rat for not telling her the truth, but the longer I waited the less I could bear to do it. I told myself that I would come clean once and for all when the show was over. Until then, Macie always seemed to have things to do with the rest of the cast, which I didn't mind too much. It meant I didn't have to lie to her face so often, and it gave me more time to hunt for Calvin.

Just like the girl with the Rolleiflex had said, Calvin's entire apartment building was vacated. When I drove by, which was at least once a day, all I ever saw were trucks from carpenters and contractors. I did, though, manage to find Calvin's car. It was parked around the corner, and was building up a fine layer of twigs and tree sap. I tried to think about what that meant. The first possibility was that he could be dead. Dead men don't move their cars. This was terrifying, but I didn't think it was true. First of all, I didn't want it to be true. Secondly, there would have been some mention of it in the paper or on TV if they'd found a charred body in the middle of that freakishly burned apartment. So, assuming he was still alive, he was around here somewhere. He couldn't get very far without a car. Unless someone else had driven him somewhere. Or something had carried him off on its leathery wings. I kept chewing over the possibilities in my mind, but they didn't lead me anywhere new.

I would drive past St. Mark's, too, but all I ever saw were industrial-cleanup vans and a few cars that looked perfectly mundane, with no SMRC stickers in sight. I emailed a couple of the addresses I found on the website of the Lamasco SMRC chapter, but nobody ever responded.

Eventually, it was time for the musical's last performance. I went to see it, not just because I was a dutiful boyfriend and a fan of live theater, but also because it was cool and dark. After the big storms, a wave of heat and humidity had rolled in, the kind that makes you feel twenty pounds heavier just by walking out the door, and turns breathing into an effort. The air conditioning at home had gone on the fritz that morning, so I was looking for somewhere to hide.

I was more relaxed than I had been on opening night, so I was able to sit back and watch the show a bit. The cast seemed different somehow, I thought. I'm not going to pretend I can detect the subtleties of a performance and how they change from night to night, but something had changed from the first time I saw them. There was an energy that pushed them forward. Not that they were rushing—it was more like they could see the finish line and were determined to use up all their energy by the time they got there.

They were good, too. I had to admit that, whatever else John Graze was—warlock, crazy guy, et cetera—he knew how to get people to perform on stage. Everybody up there: Macie, Micah Tomey, the rest of the leads, all the way down to William and the chorus, none of them seemed like high school kids playing parts. They seemed like rock stars. Once again, I wished I was up there with them.

When it was over, the audience of relatives, boyfriends, girlfriends, teachers, and people with broken air conditioners and nothing else to do, gave them a good long standing ovation. Flowers were distributed, the director and crew took bows, the orchestra peered sheepishly over the edge of the pit, and it was all over. John Graze was nowhere to be seen. I met Macie when the rest of the cast, laughing with relief, emerged from the stage doors, and we went to the cast party.

The party was at Micah's house. The house was big, and the neighbors also had kids in the cast, so no one was likely to complain too much about anything a couple dozen drama club kids might get up to. On the way there, I had expected Macie to pepper me with questions about Calvin, but she stayed off of the subject. Instead, the talk was about the normal after-show subjects: what had gone well, what had been a disaster, and who had done what to whom backstage.

When we arrived, it was clear within a few minutes that this was going to be an evening with a fair amount of tension. Fights were already starting to break out. Now, when I say "fights," I don't mean the kind of fights that happen when football players have parties (so I'm told). There were no black eyes, no bloody noses, nobody formed a circle around a couple of drunks, chanting "Fight! Fight!" None of that. When I say "fight," I mean tears, bitter denunciations in full earshot of everyone in the kitchen, one hard slap and various whispered conversations in bathrooms. Hardcore, that's what we are.

It wasn't too unusual to see this kind of thing going on. After all, the transition from "play" relationships to "real" ones was awkward, as difficult to navigate as a frozen sidewalk. But it did seem strange that it was happening so quickly. Usually at cast parties, people are still too high on applause to give much thought to breaking up, and that tends to happen in private over the next couple of agonizing weeks. Things were moving a lot faster here, and I was reminded of why that might be when William handed me a big black book, full of blank pages, for me to sign.

Apparently, that's how most of the cast were using the books John Graze had given them. William's book already had several pages of tributes written in it, the same sort of comments that you get in a yearbook, but more emotionally overwrought and frequently more vulgar. Several of the girls from the bohemian chorus had put lipstick prints on some of his pages, as well as elaborate half-joking propositions. I shook my head. William was a gawky six-four and looked like the statue outside every Big Boy restaurant. Plus, I didn't even think he liked girls. How did he do it?

I flipped to the front and saw the column of thick black runes that ran down the inside cover. I ran my fingers down them and, God as my witness, they felt warm.

I tasted blood all of a sudden and had to fight the urge to throw the damn thing out the window.

William saw me studying the book with what must have seemed like intense curiosity. "I can't believe he gave them to everyone," William said. "They're super expensive."

"He probably thought it was worth it," I said, scribbling something on a blank page and handing it back to him.

" 'Run like hell?' " William read.

"I'll explain later."

The more I saw the rest of the cast passing around their occult time bombs, the more worried I got. I went to go find Macie, who had been dragged off into a tearful bathroom conversation within the first minute.

I caught up with her upstairs in the den, where a bunch of the leads had clustered around a TV to watch the movie version of *Rent*. Mr. Fanshaw had warned them, on pain of death, to stay away from that movie during rehearsal. He hadn't wanted anyone to base their performance on aping their character in the film, but now that everything was over, the cast was having fun by watching the movie and seeing how much better they'd done.

Can you tell I'm stalling? I'm not very proud of the things that happened next. When I went into the den, Macie was sitting next to Micah on the couch. Tall, handsome Micah, who can really sing and really act and doesn't have weird hobbies like constantly taking people's pictures with old junk cameras. He had his arm around her, more or less. It was that same "Hey, my arm's just stretched out along the top of the sofa and you just happen to be sitting next to me, and the next time we laugh about something, my arm's going to accidentally slip down and around your shoulders" trick that most of us have used at some point. I stood there for a second or two to make sure I was seeing what I thought I was seeing.

"Macie, can I talk to you?"

She glanced from the TV to me to, I swear, Micah. "Can you hold on for a minute? My scene's almost on."

"It's just for a second," I said.

"Shh!" said one of the figures sprawled on the floor. This was Petey, the guy who played Angel and honestly one of the nicest people on the planet. Like, Eagle-Scout, read-to-the-elderly nice. But at that moment, all I wanted to do was kick him in the head. I felt like the entire room was staring at me as I edged over to the couch. In the back of my mind I wondered if anyone was messing around with the air conditioning. It felt a lot hotter than it had before. My upper lip was starting to sweat, which I hated.

"Please, can you just come with me?" I asked. "It's about... you know." I felt the need to wink theatrically, but I knew there was no way Micah would either miss it or refrain from commenting about it.

"In a minute, Hal," Macie said.

"You look stressed. Did you get a drink? There's stuff downstairs if you want it." Micah made a vague gesture toward the rest of the house. And there it was. The arm had gone from the sofa to the shoulders. Could it have been perfectly innocent? Could it have been a natural byproduct of two people sitting on a sofa repositioning themselves in the face of a possibly unhinged person who had just invaded their personal space? Yes, it could have been. But it wasn't. I knew.

I felt my jaw hanging open and shut it with a click. Why was this happening? I wanted to remind her that, after all, *I* was the one who had risked my life to break into a dangerous maniac's house, just to see if there was anything *I* could do for her possessed sister, who wouldn't even have been in that predicament in the first place if she'd been a better skater. Was it too much to ask that she not publicly make out with some other guy while I was right there?

"Come on," I said to Macie. I put my hand on her arm and gripped a little. Not hard, but I couldn't think of any other way to show I was serious outside of bursting into tears.

"Just calm down, all right?" Micah sat up straighter. Without moving the arm in question.

"I am calm," I said. Angrily.

"It's okay," Macie said to Micah, who had been about to stand up. I don't know what would have happened next, but I was confident it would have involved me getting punched. Strangely, I didn't care.

"All right, Hal. Fine." Macie lifted herself off of the couch.

"I'll be right back," she said over her shoulder as we left the room. I didn't look back, because I knew he would have been watching us, and I didn't want to see his face.

I half-dragged Macie down the stairs, as fast as I possibly could. I wanted to find someplace private. Not an easy task. The kitchen had a couple of sophomore girls getting alarmingly drunk, and in the living room they were watching *The Rocky Horror Picture Show* and acting out the underwear scenes. The garage was full of crew people smoking weed. I had no desire to open any door that was closed, since I could guess why it was closed in the first place. We eventually stopped at the front porch, which was temporarily unoccupied.

"Hal, what the hell is the matter with you?" Macie began.

"Me? What were you doing with Micah?"

"We were watching TV, Hal. People watch TV. It doesn't mean anything."

I pressed the heels of my hands into my eyes. It was hard to think out here. It was so hot. I told myself to focus. Maybe I was getting bent out of shape for nothing. I couldn't tell. Either way, we could argue later. Right now we had another problem.

"We have to talk about those notebooks," I said. "I think they're active now, or they're doing their thing, or whatever you want to call it."

"That's it? That's what you're overreacting about?"

"I'm not overreacting." After everything she'd seen, I couldn't believe what she was saying. "Something very weird is happening tonight. Don't tell me you don't notice it. I almost got in a fight with Micah a minute ago. Do you think that's normal?"

"Of course not."

"Thank you."

"Micah would have beaten you to death, Hal. I thought you'd gone insane."

I sputtered, but let it pass. "The runes are causing it, Macie, and it's going to get worse."

She shrugged. "It's a cast party. I think you're being paranoid."

Before I could argue this, Lacey Kumar banged through the door and onto the porch.

"Macie! Sign my book!" she trilled, and shoved the book into Macie's hands, heedless of the murderous look I was directing toward her.

Lacey had played Macie's character's love interest. She had amazing dark eyes and straight black hair that shined in the yellow porch light. It was funny that I had never noticed how beautiful she was before. I mean, she looked fine from the stage, but here, eighteen inches away, it was something else entirely. I found myself wanting to reach out to her.

I pinched myself. Something tugged at my mind for an instant, then it was gone.

"Hey, can I see that?" I asked when Macie had filled half a page. I flipped to the front and looked at the column of runes. I could feel heat through the leather cover.

"Look at these," I said to Macie.

She glanced down at the open book. "Look at what?"

I didn't know what to say. I couldn't tell if she was winding me up because I was getting on her nerves, or if she actually couldn't see them anymore.

"You mean those rune things, right?" she said. "I guess they weren't in all the books. They're not in this one."

"What are you two talking about?" Lacey asked. After a long few seconds of me sitting in shocked silence, and Macie glaring back with annoyance, Lacey lifted the book out of my hands.

"Whatever," she said, and stalked back into the house.

The slam of the door snapped me back into action. I took Macie's hand. She twitched, but didn't pull it away.

"We need to go," I said. "We can figure out what to do in the morning, but we shouldn't be here now." I stood up and tried to pull her with me.

"No."

"What?"

"I'm not going, Hal. I think you're being crazy. I just got through working with these people for a long time, and some of them I may never see again. I want to stay here for a while."

"Look…" Which is how I begin when I'm not sure what to say next.

"I understand, Hal. I really do. You're on the outside looking in. You weren't part of the show. It's natural to feel a little jealous. But I'm going to stay here for a while. I'm having fun."

That was it. For a second, I thought about punching her in the jaw, knocking her unconscious, and carrying her off over my shoulder. I didn't, though. As agitated as I was, I was still pretty sure it wouldn't work in real life the way it did in the movies, no matter how much I wanted it to. Then I thought about just leaving, about letting her stay here like she said she wanted. Maybe nothing bad would happen.

I sighed. The only thing I could do was try, so I looked Macie in the eye and made an effort to put all the panic and bad feelings of the night out of my mind. "Macie, I know you don't want to go, but I'm begging you. I can't explain it in a way that'll make sense to you now, but

I will later, I promise. Just take it on faith this time. That's all I can ask. If I mean anything to you, come with me. Please." There it was. The if-you-love-me-you'll-do-it-for-me ploy. The relationship nuclear option. The big test. I waited for a couple of seconds, not knowing what was going to happen next.

Macie stood up. "All right," she said.

She wasn't happy about it, and her body language made sure I knew it, but she followed me to my car. In the driveway, we passed William, who had his arms around two shorter members of the chorus and an expression of glee on his face.

"You're leaving?" he asked.

I nodded. "Come with us." It felt like I was swimming against a strong current, but the car was only a few feet away.

William snorted and whispered something to the chorister on his left, who giggled and the three of them went off into the house. I thought about running after him, but I knew that if I took a step in that direction, I would lose Macie, too. So we kept going.

Macie didn't speak to me on the drive to her house, and she got out of the car before I could try to kiss her goodnight. All the way home I felt like I'd made the wrong choice, but at the same time I couldn't think of anything else I might have done. I fell asleep and had horrible nightmares, but couldn't remember any of them when I woke up.

173

10

The next morning my parents woke me up and dragged me off to Mass at St. John's. I would have preferred sleeping in, but what can I do? I'm a good son. Besides, after a few weeks of warlocks, unnatural lightning storms, monsters, and cast parties, a little church didn't sound like a bad idea.

The southern part of Indiana had a huge wave of German Catholic immigrants in the decades before World War I, so every little town on the map around here has its own Catholic church. Lamasco itself has at least a dozen. St. John's, which was ours, used to be a little black box church attended by farmers and coal miners, but it was rebuilt in the Eighties and lost all its character. I would have preferred going to one of the really old churches downtown, but that would have meant getting up a lot earlier. As much as I love old things, there are limits.

During Mass my mind drifted, as it tends to do, and I wondered if it would do any good to talk to the priest about what was going on with John Graze, Calvin, Macie, the monsters, and me. After all, if this stuff was really happening, you'd think the Church would know something about it. Then again, I wasn't sure if I could bring myself to take it up with Father Carl. He was a decent guy, but it was pretty clear that St. John's was his last stop before heading off to the retired priests' home. Springing an honest-to-God manifestation of the powers of darkness on him just seemed cruel.

When I got home, I called Macie. Her phone rang a couple of times and I imagined all kinds of dire situations for the thirty seconds it took for her to pick up.

"Hello?"

"Hey, it's me. How are you feeling?"

"I've been better. My head hurts. I feel hung over, but I wasn't at the party long enough to drink that much."

"Yeah, about that," I said. "Listen..."

She interrupted me. "Hal, it's okay. I don't know what happened. I was just pissed off, and everything we said to each other just seemed to make it worse. I don't know. I'm sorry."

"That's all right," I said.

"I don't know why I was acting like that." She stopped for a second, then said, "Well, I guess I do."

"Yeah. I think whatever those runes are supposed to do, they're starting to do it. Is it okay if I come over?

175

I've got some other things you probably ought to know about."

"Give me about an hour, okay? I just woke up."

"Sure."

"Hal?"

"Yes?"

"Thanks for not walking out on me."

"Don't worry about it. Everyone was a little wound up last night. Me included."

"I'm really sorry. I mean it," Macie said.

"No problem. Hey—What are you wearing?"

"Hmm... Panties and a pair of mirrored sunglasses."

"You're the best. See you in a bit."

When I got over there, Macie, wearing the sunglasses but fully dressed, led me to the back porch. We looked out at the fake lake in the center of her housing development and drank lemonade while I told her the story of the fires at the SMRC headquarters and Calvin's apartment. It didn't take long to tell, but by the time I was done I was holding her hand tightly.

"So that's it," I said. "Calvin is gone. Unless we want to try finding another SMRC chapter in a different city or something, I think we're on our own."

Macie swirled the ice around in the bottom of her glass. "Maybe not. You said Calvin's car is still there, so I don't think he got chased away. And I don't think he got killed, either."

"Really?" I said, unbelieving. I had begun to accept the idea that Calvin had completely vaporized, so this sounded like pointless optimism to me.

"I know a little bit about how Mr. Graze thinks," Macie said. "He likes to do things his way. When we were doing the show, he would give way more specific directions than Mr. Fanshaw ever would. He'd never explain or tell us why we were doing something. He would just be like, 'Step here, turn this much, look that way, hit the syllables there and there.' Then we'd do it and it would actually make a great sequence, and we would understand what he was talking about. It was like he needed us to see that he was right, that his ideas were the best ones. I think it's the same thing here. If he wanted to kill Calvin or the rest of the SMRC people, he'd do it. But he doesn't want to. He wants this whole process to work out the way he set it up. It's his performance."

"His last Left Hand Ritual album," I said. "*Lords of Air and Darkness*. The one he never got to finish." I began to understand where she was coming from. Personally, I had been in half a dozen plays over the past few years and had never gotten to know a director well enough to be able to predict what they might do in civilian life, but I knew a little bit about John Graze. And I knew Macie was right. This made sense. His plan was unfolding, and Calvin was probably still around somewhere, hiding, frightened, and without his car. All we had to do was find him.

So we went looking.

That night, after work, Macie met me outside the restaurant and we drove to where Calvin's car was parked. The sky was a dark purple, almost black. Fortunately, Calvin's car was under a streetlight.

"Look at that," Macie said as she shined a flashlight in through the window. "That is a lot of junk in one car."

I was distracted by heat-lightning flashes in the clouds overhead. I wondered if that signified more bad weather tomorrow. Macie tried both door handles on her side and motioned me around to check the others. The wind had picked up and the limbs of the tree overhead had begun to creak. All of a sudden, I was nervous. My heart was beating so loud, it was probably audible across the street. I hadn't been this spooked when I had been in John Graze's inner sanctum, taking pictures. Why was I so scared to be messing with a parked car on a quiet street?

"Let me check something." Macie crouched by the front fender, reaching around for something underneath. Somewhere close by, a night bird called. With a triumphant expression, she stood up and held out a little magnetized key-holder box.

"Toss it over here," I said. "I'll do the trunk first." As I put the key in the trunk lock, I wondered if *this* was where Calvin had disappeared to. Cautiously, I took a deep breath of fresh air and pressed the latch button.

It swung up agonizingly slowly, to reveal… very little.

"Are you kidding me?" I said to the universe.

Calvin's trunk was pristine. Showroom clean, almost.

"How does somebody with that much garbage in his back seat have nothing in his trunk?" Macie asked.

"If it's in the back seat, you can reach for it while you're driving," I offered. I made a mental note to vacuum out my car when I got the chance. It wasn't as bad as Calvin's yet, but I imagined it was a slippery slope.

"What's that?"

Macie's flashlight had revealed a dark green canvas bag lurking in the back corner of the trunk. "Hey, I remember this." I reached for it. "That's—"

The night bird called again. It sounded like it was right above us. Before the echoes of its cry died down, there was another sound from the branches overhead. It was laughter. Macie twitched the flashlight beam up into the tree.

"God!" I choked.

Crouched on a sturdy limb, ten feet above our head, was the blonde girl I had seen coming out of Calvin's building. She still wore the same white shirt and purple shorts, and she had on the same round sunglasses.

She grinned down at us. "What'dja find?" she asked.

Her feet were bare. Her toes were unnaturally long, and the big toes bent under to grip the branch like a claw. The toenails were ragged, dirty points.

My chest felt cold. I wondered if I was going to faint. I was certain she was about to jump down from that tree at any second, and I didn't want to imagine what she would do next. So I did the first thing that came to mind: I grabbed Macie's hand and the bag from Calvin's trunk and raced to my car.

"What was that?" Macie asked as we sped away.

"I don't know. I don't want to find out."

"Did you see her feet?"

"Yeah."

My headlights lit up a tall man with gray hair, standing on the corner. He was probably just walking to the coffee house, but in my heightened state of nerves he looked a lot like John Graze. He watched the car as it passed by, and I tried to keep from shivering. I concentrated on my driving. We drove past the cathedral where my rich cousins got married. We drove past the old Victorian post office and the blocky office buildings. Past the Art Deco Greyhound bus station, which I'd taken a dozen pictures of. Anyone in Lamasco who owned a camera had taken pictures of the bus station at some point. It was a city ordinance. We drove under the expressway and passed Willard Library, and I began to feel a little more normal.

Macie unzipped the bag and looked inside.

"That's a ladder," I explained to her, since she was clearly puzzled about what the assemblage of chain, rods, and hooks could be. I explained how we'd used it to get over John Graze's wall.

"It's brand new," she commented. "The wrapping is still in here. And the receipt." She held it up to the light as we passed a gas station. "Army Surplus Unlimited."

"That's the one on First Avenue, right?"

"So it says. I think we just passed it," Macie said. "Maybe they remember Calvin. He's not an easy person to forget."

I thought back to our adventure breaking into John Graze's house. "I bet they probably do know him. Calvin said his friend gave him a good deal on the ladder."

"We can go back tomorrow when the store's open," Macie said. "That sounds like a better idea than checking Calvin's car again. Let's give whatever's hanging out there some time to go away."

"Good idea. Here, I've got something for you." I dug into my pocket and took out the little paper scroll that Calvin had given me earlier. I'd kept it around my neck for a while, but it made me feel like an idiot and I was always afraid I'd spill something on it or I'd sweat too much and it would disintegrate. So I'd wrapped the cord around it a few times to form a tiny little bound-up package, like a mummified beetle, and kept in it my pocket.

Macie cautiously undid the cord and let it spin freely. I explained that Calvin had said it was a protective magical thingy, and it might have been why I hadn't been affected by the weird magic at the cast party last night.

"Just don't untie the thread that holds the paper together. That's part of the magic, I think. And make sure you don't eat it."

"I'm glad you told me that. It was the first thing I was going to do the minute your back was turned."

"I figured. Anyway, I thought you ought to have it."

We drove past the city pool where I had taken swimming lessons a long time ago. All of a sudden, I wished I could ride on the concrete dolphin outside the entrance again, the way I used to when I was a little kid.

"If I have this, what are you going to do?" Macie asked as she put the cord around her neck.

"Me? I'll just stay close to you." I reached out and put my hand on her thigh.

The next morning, when I went to pick up Macie, she ran out of her house and jumped into the car before I could even turn off the engine.

"Hi," she said.

"Hi yourself. Aren't you going to be hot in that?" She was wearing a thick flannel shirt that would have been more appropriate, perhaps even a bit much, if we'd been running away to become lumberjacks.

"Just drive."

When we pulled away from her house, she unbuttoned her shirt and threw it into the back seat. Underneath, she wore a green tank top with a deep V-neck. A surprisingly deep V-neck. She didn't usually show a whole lot of cleavage, but it looked like today was going to be different.

"What?" she asked, as I continued to stare.

"Do you want to drive? I'm having a hard time paying attention to the road all of a sudden."

"Funny. You want me to put my shirt back on?"

"I do not." I jammed on the brakes to make a rapidly-approaching stop light. I wasn't kidding about the paying-attention thing. Of all the days to leave my camera at home.

"This is a new look, isn't it?" I asked.

"I thought it would be helpful. If we're going to talk to a bunch of store clerks, I thought I could make them want to help us."

"What makes you so sure we're going to be talking to guys?"

"It's an army surplus store, right? I think the odds are pretty good." She adjusted the heavily engineered bra straps under her shirt and made a lipstick-checking pout in my sun visor mirror.

"I'm the luckiest guy in the whole world," I said.

"I'm glad you realize that."

The army surplus store was in a neighborhood that grew up before everybody had cars. There were long stretches of narrow-faced houses, with no driveways in between, and factories every few blocks, which was where the people who had lived in those houses had worked. Some of the factories had been converted into new things like shops or offices, and some still looked like they made whatever it was they made eighty years ago. Others were empty and falling apart, so you couldn't quite tell if the neighborhood was just about to get better or just about to get worse.

We pulled into the store's parking lot. Fortunately, there weren't a whole lot of customers, which I thought would make it easier to talk to the clerk. I'd been in here once or twice before, to buy a backpack or a raincoat, things that looked cooler and lasted longer than what you could find at Target. There was always a little mental resistance when I got to the door. They don't present the friendliest of faces. The door was covered with stickers, including the National Rifle Association logo; a bulldog with a Marine Corps tattoo chewing on a human leg; and a sign reading "Shoplifters Will Not Live To Be Prosecuted." None of them really said "Come on in and browse!"

Inside, it looked like an attic, with rows and rows of dusty olive drab folded on shelves and hanging from racks. It had that characteristic smell that thrift stores and army surplus stores share. It felt disorganized, but with the suggestion that you could find almost anything you wanted if you were willing to look hard enough.

The clerk was a leathery older guy with a gray-streaked mustache. I sidled up to the counter right away. I was carrying Calvin's bag, so I wanted the clerk to know that I'd brought it in with me. I had a feeling they weren't kidding about the shoplifting thing.

"Hi," I said. "I wonder if I could ask you a quick question." I put the bag on the glass counter. "I went climbing with a friend of mine, and he forgot some of his stuff. I'm trying to get in touch with him so I can give it back." I unzipped the bag to show the chain ladder. "He bought it here." I showed him the receipt. "I hoped maybe you might remember him—he said he knew somebody here. His first name's Calvin, by the way," I added belatedly.

"What's his last name?" the guy asked.

"I don't know."

"He's your friend and you don't know his last name?"

"Hi!" Macie had joined us. She rested her elbows on the counter, pulled her shoulders back, and perused the display of knives under the glass. "We just met him," Macie explained. "We were at a SMRC meeting. You know, they use those fake names there? Between the two of us, we were only able to remember his real first name."

"Can you describe him?" asked the guy. All of a sudden, he was having trouble maintaining eye contact with me. Macie was leaning over the counter with all the subtlety of a Benny Hill sketch, and I half expected the guy to assume we were pulling some sort of weird con game and throw us out, but it actually worked. I suppose I shouldn't sound so surprised. I wasn't even the target and it was working on me. I pulled myself together and described Calvin to him: the size, the beard, the glasses that said "forget about the fancy stuff, show me whatever's cheap and durable." I even went so far as to imitate Calvin's unusual cadence of speech: half professor and half overgrown slacker.

Eventually, the clerk nodded. "Yeah. Calvin Ferguson. That's got to be him."

"Do you know him?"

"A little bit. Comes in here every once in a while. I see him at the Book Broker a lot. I think he works there."

"Really? Awesome. Thanks a lot." We left, but not before I bought a set of camping forks and spoons that locked together with metal pegs. I felt like we owed it to him.

"What are you going to do with those?" Macie asked me as we drove away.

"Next time we go camping, I'll be able to eat like a civilized person."

"When have we ever been camping?"

"Now that I have the right utensils, we can go all the time. Let's pitch a tent in my back yard."

Our new destination was halfway across town. I detoured through a couple of bad neighborhoods—one with good architecture and one with bad—to avoid getting close to the Alhambra Theater and what might still be lurking inside.

The Book Broker was a big, white two-story place set all by itself in a little patch of trees between strip malls. There were a couple of wings and additions attached to the main body in strange places, like it had expanded haphazardly over the years. It was the kind of place where all the windows were plastered over with giant-sized cutouts of comic book characters and posters of action movies from a decade ago. I had been here before, but I wasn't a regular customer. As someone who enjoyed the theater and vintage gizmos, I had the feeling that I was peculiar enough already without adding whatever psychic baggage attaches to you when you spend lots of time around comic books. Macie had never been, because she's a girl.

But I kid the Book Broker. It was actually a very interesting place, in the same disreputable, vaguely odd way the army surplus store was. And to be fair, if someone saw me leap on an Olympus Pen half-frame camera, labeled "Possibly Broken-$3" at a flea market, they'd probably think I was disreputable and odd, too.

We went inside. Even before the little bell over the door stopped ringing, Macie had begun to cough. Allergies. Being around six tons of slowly decaying paper was probably going to be tough on her.

"We'll be quick," I said.

"Take your—" was as far as she got before falling victim to another fit of coughing and sniffles.

Inside, there was more than just comic books. There were videos for sale, sports cards, an infinite amount of used books, role-playing games, and weird memorabilia like eighteen-inch statuettes of anime girls with cat's ears. If you were a certain type of person, the Book Broker had everything you ever needed, and most of it was used and half price.

There were a few customers here and there, sorting through boxes of comics or digging through waist-high bins marked "Used DVDs $3.99 — Two for $7.00." The guy behind the counter was extremely skinny, with a haggard expression that suggested running this place was not as easy as it looked. His hair was combed severely over to one side and he wore a Rush t-shirt.

"Hi," I said, after checking a few of the featured comics on display. "Is Calvin Ferguson around?"

The way he jumped, you would have thought I'd said something like, "Hello, I have a large quantity of explosives hidden in my pants, and the world has really been getting on my nerves today." The clerk stood straight up, as if electrified, and stared at Macie and me.

"Is there something wrong?" I asked.

"Who did you say?" he croaked. I could tell he was keeping his voice down in an effort not to alarm the customers.

"Calvin Ferguson. I thought he worked here. He's about this tall…" I described him again. I was getting good at this. If we ended up filing a missing persons report on Calvin, I was going to get along great with the police artist who did the sketch.

He nodded nervously. "Come with me," he said, and lifted the gate that separated the behind-the-counter area from the riffraff. He led us to the other side of the store, up a six-inch step and into a low-ceilinged, catacomb-like place filled with used books on rough plywood shelving.

Macie elbowed me and made a "What's going on?" face. I shrugged.

"The mysteries start back here," he said, and pointed to a spot on the floor-to-ceiling shelves. "They go all the way along there. It's not really alphabetized, but that's kind of the fun."

He sidestepped a shrunken-looking man who was peering at the three-deep stacks of paperbacks. "It's mostly science fiction over here. Science fiction and fantasy. Over there we have self-help." He pointed out different areas. "A lot of AA books and psychology. New Age and occult stuff there. General nonfiction around the corner."

The shrunken guy seemed annoyed by the clerk loudly disturbing his browsing, so he scuttled off into another part of the store. As soon as he was gone, our guide stopped talking as quickly as if someone had pressed a "mute" button. He hurried over to a brown wooden door set in a little alcove among the bookshelves. He took a key out of his pocket and looked down at us.

"Who was it again you were here to see?"

"Calvin. Calvin Ferguson." I was beginning to wonder whether it might be wise to run away from this guy.

"Okay." He unlocked the door, then reached in and switched on the light. "Here you go," he said, and stepped back.

Behind the door was a little office, hardly much bigger than a small bedroom. It had a shallow desk against one wall, a folding metal chair, and a well-used couch. Piles of papers, notebooks, binders, and hardback books were stacked up anywhere there was space.

What the room did not have was a window or another door, which was a shame because the minute Macie and I stepped inside, the guy closed the door behind us. Half a second later, we heard the sound of the key turning in the lock.

Like you'd expect, we spent the next few minutes pounding on the door and the walls, shifting back and forth between assurances that we had no hard feelings and could be reasonable, and threats to burn the place down—either with gasoline or with lawyers—if we were not freed this instant.

None of this produced any results. I wasn't surprised. I doubted this little office was soundproofed, but if I was a customer here, I'd probably ignore any muffled thumps and screams I might hear, too.

"Well, I think we're stuck." I massaged my hand, which had gotten sore from the pounding.

Macie rattled the doorknob again, just in case. The knob was all scratched up on our side, and the unlocking button had been replaced by a round metal plate.

"I can't believe this!"

"I know," I said. "Who would have thought a Rush fan would do something like this?"

"Now, Hal? Music jokes? Really?"

"Sorry."

"What are we supposed to do?" she asked.

I sighed. "I don't know."

Now that the initial wave of panic had passed, we took a look around the area where future demolitions workers might find our skeletons. There was dust on the papers that covered the desk, as well as on the handful of knickknacks that stuck up here and there through the disorder.

"What *is* all this stuff?" Macie sorted through the pages. Some were handwritten, and others were neatly typed on an old-fashioned typewriter. I could feel the impressions on the back of the paper that each individual key had left. Many of them had diagrams: columns of letters and hand-drawn symbols, complicated designs that looked like ancient astronomical charts, even a few ugly primitive things like what I'd seen on the walls of John Graze's nest.

However, I was more curious about some of the other things I found on the desk. A fountain pen and a bottle of red ink. A Sony Walkman, of all things, with a tape inside labeled "Parsons Lectures." A hole punch whose cylindrical punching die had been sharpened into a rough point. A little kit of dissecting tools, which had not been cleaned in a very long time. A wooden box with a complicated knot pattern carved into the lid, and metal plates reinforcing the corners, the kind of thing you might buy as an impulse purchase at the Renaissance Faire. I picked it up. It felt heavier than I expected, given its size.

I opened the lid and screamed.

11

Okay, I didn't exactly scream. But I definitely made a loud noise of surprise and confusion. Possibly closer to a shriek. Or even a squeal. I'm just glad I didn't involuntarily throw the thing across the room. Inside the box was a tiny model of an office, just like the one we were trapped in. There was a tiny chair, a bite-sized couch, and a little desk strewn with papers smaller than a fingernail. What had scared me was the fact that something alive was scampering around in there. At first, I thought it was a mangy white mouse. Then I looked closer.

"Calvin?"

He stared up at me, smaller than the Star Wars guys I used to play with years ago.

"Hal, is that you?" His voice sounded distant and hollow, like he was yelling up from the bottom of a deep well. I was a little surprised that he didn't sound like a cartoon character, all squeaky and sped-up.

I heard a gasp. Macie had looked over my shoulder to see where the voice had come from. "What is that?" she whispered.

"Hi there! Make yourselves comfortable," Calvin said. "I think there's some cereal in the desk drawer if you're hungry."

We cleared a little space on the edge of the desk and set the box on it. We looked down at tiny Calvin and tiny Calvin looked up at us.

"So how'd you guys find me?" Calvin asked.

"Well, first—" I said.

"Calvin, what happened to you?" Macie interrupted.

Calvin hauled his tiny bulk onto the couch. "Can you hear me all right? It's hard to tell sometimes. Okay, how did I get here? Well, when I was very young I was always interested in magic..."

I tapped the corner of the box with an impatient finger.

"Sorry. Kidding. I've been in here a long time. You two are the first people I've talked to in—what has it been? A week? A month? I think I'm a little stir crazy."

"Just take it slow. Tell us what happened." Macie was trying hard to sound reasonable, which I appreciated. As for myself, I was beginning to think that we were stuck in a box of our own, and I wanted to have an answer ready when somebody lifted the roof off and asked me the same questions we were asking Calvin.

"Remember the day we got into John Graze's house?" Calvin asked.

"As a matter of fact, I do," I said.

"Remember the storm? Well, right after I dropped you off at your car, I started to suspect it wasn't just a natural storm."

"How did you know?"

"John's face appeared on my windshield and promised me an eternity of torment if I didn't leave him alone."

I had to agree. That did not sound like a normal weather phenomenon.

"Something must have alerted him that we were in his house," Calvin said. "Some spell, or a pair of eyes watching us from a corner we didn't check. Fortunately, all his guard could do was warn him, so we were pretty lucky."

"Yeah." I glanced from the locked door to the tiny man trapped in the wooden box. "I'm glad we didn't end up with any *real* problems."

"When I got back to my apartment, I tried to call you, but I realized I didn't have your number. I checked the directory, but there were a lot of Hugheses in there, and I didn't even know if you lived in town or not. I went to call Brocelinde from SMRC to see if she had your name on the sign-up sheet, but the phone was suddenly dead. Then the power went out."

Calvin paused while I pulled up a chair for Macie to sit on and I perched on the edge of the desk.

"I was sitting on the couch in my apartment, in the pitch darkness with lightning flashing around outside, trying to decide what to do next. That's when the door to my kitchen opened all by itself. Behind it was a sheet of flame. I thought one of my old power strips had finally blown up, but then the flame moved. It walked toward me. As I watched, the fire took the shape of a man, this mass of orange flame with two blue-white circles for eyes. It looked at me as it walked and I could tell there was an evil intelligence behind it. Wherever it stepped, flames sprang up behind it. It didn't make a sound, but I knew what it wanted. There was no way it would let me leave the room alive. That's when I spoke the word of return."

"What's that?" Macie asked before I could.

"Everyone who uses magic eventually discovers that it's useful to be able to get away from someplace in a hurry." Calvin was starting to sound less like a man trapped in a box and more like a teacher expounding on his favorite subject. "There are lots of reasons: an angry mob, a failed experiment, a natural disaster, or, in this case, a creature summoned by a rival wizard. Now, the problem is that magic is often a slow process. You've seen that yourselves: If John Graze could have carried out his plans by snapping his fingers, he would have. Instead, it's taken him months to set up his spells just right. To have an instant escape route, you have to prepare much of it beforehand, and then when you need it, all you have to do is say the 'word of return,' the last piece that completes the transformation. Then—bang!—you're there. I had set up my spell to return me to my office. Toby, the owner of the place—he's the one who probably locked you in here—he lets me keep this office to do research and work on some of my magical experiments. I hate to do that kind of thing at home, since it tends to produce some weird vibrations."

"And nobody's going to notice that here?" I asked.

"Surprisingly, no. Second-hand possessions, especially books, have their own vibrations, so nobody notices a little more."

Calvin tapped the wall of his box. From our side, it sounded like a hollow knock, like somebody dropping a marble inside. "As you can tell, something went wrong. I honestly don't know what it was. I could have done something wrong when I set up the first part of the spell. Or something may have gone off, decayed a little, over time. It was years ago when I set this up, and I really never got around to checking it. Or I could have done the word of return wrong. I was a little distracted by the fire monster. It's funny: You prepare and you make a plan and you tell yourself you know what you have to do and how you'll do it, but when the time comes, your mind's a blank."

"Well, I'm glad you were able to get this far, at least," I said. "How do we get you out of there?"

197

"Good question."

"You don't know?" Macie asked.

"It took me a whole day to figure out where I was. All I knew at first was that the door was stuck and that these—" he waved two handfuls of paper "—were unreadable gibberish. Then I realized that the smell I'd been smelling since I arrived was wood stain and the illusion began to fade. Once I knew where I was, all I had to do was wait for someone to show up and rescue me."

"Yeah, about that," I said. "We're kind of locked in here."

"All part of the emergency escape plan. I told Toby that if I ever didn't show up for a few days and then somebody came in asking for Calvin Ferguson, to take them in here and lock the door. The lock is closed by magic. It's a pretty simple spell, but it's strong enough to keep people out. Or in. If they were friends of mine, looking in my papers for clues about what happened to me, then they should also have enough magic to get themselves out. If they were the ones who had caused my disappearance in the first place, then the door would slow them down long enough for my own magical protector to deal with them." He pointed over our heads, to where a small taxedermied bat clung to the ceiling. Its eyes glowed bright green, which should have been impossible in this light.

"So anybody who came in here and asked for Calvin Ferguson would have gotten locked in this office?" Macie sounded shocked at the inefficiency of it all.

"Yep. My real name's Calvin Hyde. I only use the other name when I'm working with magic."

"How many names do you have?" Macie asked.

"Now that you mention it, a lot. It happens. Wizards tend to end up with a bunch of names."

"Don't get me wrong, this is all fascinating," I said, "but could you tell us how to get out of here?" I hated the idea of being locked in this room and unable to get out. The walls weren't beginning to close in on me, but they were definitely inching in that direction.

Tiny Calvin sighed a tiny sigh. "I was wondering when you were going to ask about that."

"I don't like the sound of this," I said.

"Here's the deal—"

"Oh, no," Macie said.

"Remember how I said the door was locked with magic?"

"All right, so it's a spell," I said. "Undo it."

Macie's face lit up with sudden understanding. "I know what Calvin means," she said. "He can't. Calvin, you can't do any magic while you're in the box, can you?"

"I can do plenty. All I want. It just doesn't affect anything outside of the box." He muttered something under his breath and the inside of the box was filled with tiny glowing lights that floated in the air like paper lanterns.

"Very impressive." I could hear the anxiety in my voice. "What are we supposed to do now?"

"I need you to look around the office for a paper with this diagram written on it." Calvin rooted around in his miniature desk and pulled out a marker, which he used to draw some shapes on the wall of his box. It was a wheel divided up into several segments by long lines topped with looping squiggles. Geometric figures were impaled on the lines at different places throughout the drawing.

We finally found it in the snowdrift of papers on the desk. It was a photocopy of something, which Calvin had then traced over with a green marker. On the back were long blocks of handwritten notes, which I was unable to read.

"It's my own script," Calvin explained. "I invented it myself. The alphabet, at least. The actual grammar is pretty similar to English, but I made some adjustments."

"So you're the only one who can read all of this?" Macie asked as she squinted at the paper.

"More or less. It's sort of a wizard's tradition. When you have to translate something into another language, you understand it better. But don't worry, you don't have to read very much of it to learn the spell."

So he taught us. It's hard to describe what happened, mostly because I never ended up being any good at it, but he told us to visualize building that wheel-shape in our minds, each segment appearing in a particular order. At the same time, we were supposed to recite the syllables of a long phrase that sounded like nonsense, timing each syllable with the appearance of each segment. Actually, we weren't supposed to *say* the syllables, we just had to *hear* them in our heads.

"The thing to remember is that these energies are all around us," our miniature guru said. "We just have to contact them in the right order and at the right time."

Nothing happened on our first few tries. Calvin said he could tell we were improving with each attempt, but I suspected he was just trying to keep our spirits up. We kept at it, though, taking turns trying to get through the routine with enough concentration or purity of heart or whatever the hell it was supposed to take to get that door open. I glanced over at Macie. Her eyes were closed and her lips were twitching. I could tell she was running through the syllables. I was surprised that she had jumped into this so completely. Even after all I'd seen and all the monsters that had tried to eat me, I still had to force myself to believe that whatever we were doing could actually have some effect on the door in front of us.

I was practicing for my next attempt, alternating my attention between the diagram, the syllables, and a cheat sheet I'd written for myself, when I heard a soft metallic *ting*. I looked up and the door to the office had swung open half a foot.

201

I stared at Macie. "I did it!" she said. She wore a big surprised grin, as if he'd just developed, well, magic powers.

While we shared a victory hug, Calvin said, "Congratulations! Now, I need you to go and find someone from SMRC. One of them should be able to get me out of here."

"What about us?" I asked. I was apparently on a contact high from Macie's success. "What kind of spell will get you out? Can you teach it to us?"

Calvin scratched his beard. "Don't take this the wrong way, but I'd just as soon have someone from SMRC do it."

"We got the door open, didn't we?" I asked.

"The door wasn't going to spend eternity in the lost spaces between the dimensions if you got the spell wrong."

"I see your point," Macie said. "We'll find the SMRC people for you."

"Are you going to be okay in there? Do you need anything?" I asked. "Tiny magazine? Thimble of water?"

"You're very funny. No. Just close the lid. It changes the way time passes in here, I think."

"What about the door? Is it going to lock again?"

"It's a tough spell. It'll be fine, even after everything you two did to it. Even if it isn't, it won't be any problem for the others."

We slipped out of the office and through the store, past Toby the manager, who still looked at us like we were radioactive. When we got in the car, Macie leaned over and kissed me. She was beaming.

"What?" I asked.

"I did magic."

I nodded. That was about all I could do. "Yes, you did."

Neither of us wanted to hurry home, so I cruised a wandering course through the neighborhood streets instead of taking the direct route to Macie's subdivision. I think we both wanted to enjoy a little bit of freedom after having been stuck in that office. I hoped Calvin would be okay until we could find someone to set him loose. He had seemed as sane as he'd ever been, but that wasn't saying much.

When we got to Macie's house, her mother was waiting for us on the porch.

"Where have you been?" she demanded of Macie, as soon as we got out of the car. Mrs. Hart's voice sounded tight, as if she had to fight to get the words out without shouting. This was the first time I had ever seen her mother unhappy, and it freaked me out a little.

"Mom, what's the matter?"

"I've been calling and calling you. Why didn't you answer?"

Macie checked her phone. Fourteen messages. "I must have been somewhere with a bad signal. Sorry, Mom. What happened?"

"Two girls from the play—Sonia Greene and Lacey Kumar. Have you seen them?"

Macie shook her head. "What's going on?"

"They're missing!"

"What happened?" I asked. Mrs. Hart shot me a look, and I realized she may have had other ideas as to why Macie hadn't been checking her phone. I tried to look innocent.

"Sonia's mother called me," Mrs. Hart said to Macie, as if Macie had asked the question. "She's been calling everyone that Sonia might know. She says they had a huge fight, then Sonia—I can hardly believe this— destroyed their television, then ran away with their car."

"Mom, that's nuts," Macie said. "Sonia wouldn't do that." She hesitated. "Probably not."

I knew Sonia slightly, and I privately thought she would lean more toward locked doors and sleeping pills if she wanted to make trouble. But I didn't say anything. It was clear that Mrs. Hart was in no mood to hear my opinions.

Macie started to say something else, then stopped herself. I could tell what she was thinking about: The leather book that had probably been on Sonia's dresser, and the line of runes inside it. Sonia may not have been capable of property damage and grand theft, but the thing those runes had attracted surely was.

"After that, Sonia drove over to the other girl's house. What was her name? Lacey. Apparently, when Sonia got there, she drove her car across their lawn and *into the pool.*"

I stood there and tried to act surprised. Macie shot me a side-eye look, which was all she could do in front of her nearly hyperventilating mother.

"Then Lacey ran outside, pulled Sonia out of the car, and they ran away into the woods. Nobody knows where they've gone. Can you imagine what would have made them act that way?"

We shook our heads. What good would it have done to tell the truth?

"Sonia's mother doesn't think it's drugs, but..." Mrs. Hart shrugged. "What else could it be? I was so worried when I couldn't reach you." She threw her arms around Macie. "I'm just glad you're back."

I quietly stepped away.

12

As I drove home, Sonia and Lacey were on my mind. Had they seen the creatures? Were they aware of what was happening to them? I had a hard time thinking about it. Whenever I tried, my thoughts slipped away to some other topic. It was like trying to grab a wet balloon. I didn't feel right. I kept adjusting the air conditioning and couldn't get it set to a temperature I liked.

When I pulled into the driveway, I heard the sound of a table saw and knew that my dad was working in the garage. A long time ago, our house had been part of a dairy farm. Because of that, there were a handful of barns, garages, and outbuildings around the main house. Dad had taken over the nearest one for his large array of woodworking gear, and we parked the cars wherever we could find space. My mom was digging in one of the sandstone-bordered flower beds that circled the house. It was one of those summer evenings when the shadows have fallen but it's still light out, giving everything the rich, warm colors of an old National Geographic photo.

It was finally starting to cool down a little. Bugs were singing in the trees and I felt like sitting in one of the chairs on the porch and watching the twilight grow, but I had to balance that against the possibility that one of my parents might notice me and ask me to help with something. My parents were project people. They were never happier than when they were doing something. I preferred to do nothing. This difference in philosophy had caused much discussion in the past. I took a deep breath of air, which had the scent of honeysuckle in it, then sneaked inside. I got a glass of orange juice and went upstairs to my room.

I scanned the row of cameras on my shelf. They looked down at me like one-eyed mutant puppies, all wanting to be picked up and played with. It was times like these that I felt like an idiot for having so many. Eventually I picked up my Holga and loaded it with some film from my desk drawer. I was running low. It was probably time to make a run downtown to Risley's Camera and pick up more. I kept hoping that the grizzled old owner would eventually develop a soft spot in his heart for the kid who still shoots with film, and give me a discount on supplies. It hadn't happened yet, but it had to eventually. I would wear him down.

In the drawer I saw the file of negatives I'd taken when Calvin and I were in John Graze's house, and copies of the prints. All of a sudden, I felt like tearing them up and burning the pieces. Why did this have to be my problem? I was perfectly happy living my dumb little life with my records and my cameras and my girlfriend. I didn't ask for any of this. Let someone else deal with it. I couldn't.

I held the file in my hand for a second. From outside, I heard the chink of a trowel against sandstone, then the high whine of the table saw.

What else could I do? This problem wasn't going away, and no one was volunteering to take it off my hands. I fired up the computer and opened the web browser. The first thing I needed to do was find some of Calvin's friends.

The next morning I tried to call Macie, but all I got was her voicemail, so I gathered up my Holga and the address I printed out last night and drove off. The website for the Lamasco SMRC group had a list of the club officers, but they all used their made-up medieval names, which was not helpful when you were trying to find a home address. Fortunately, their membership coordinator, the woman known as Brocelinde, had also listed her real name, address, phone number, and email for the benefit of potential new members who wouldn't know who was who yet. That's where I would start.

It felt like a better idea to talk to her in person rather than call her up and babble about wizards over the phone. I found her house without any trouble. It was on Weinbach Avenue, a few blocks away from the University of Lamasco. It was a small, brick house, like most of the ones on that block. A big dogwood tree stood in the front yard, and on the porch was a concrete goose dressed in black and holding a battle-axe. I suspected I was in the right place.

When I knocked on the door, a thin man with a long mustache and round glasses answered.

I smiled. "Excuse me, I was looking for Nan Peters. Is this her house?"

"She's not here right now." The man acted like the question irritated him. "She's at a SMRC meeting."

"Oh. Is that at St. Mark's?"

He nodded, with a suspicious expression on his face. He seemed to be waiting for me to explain something or to admit that I knew some secret. It made me nervous, so I thanked him and got back in my car. As I drove, I wondered what I had done to upset him. Had I arrived too early and woken him up? That was the most likely explanation, but it also seemed like he had truly been worried about something.

With the right shortcuts, St. Mark's was only a few minutes away. This was where being a delivery boy really paid off. I could drive back and forth across the city five different ways blindfolded, and I always had a good guess about the shortest distance between any two points on the map. I almost felt bad that I didn't have any Korean food to take to the church. I hated to waste a good driving job.

There were a lot of cars in the parking lot when I got there, and a number of them had bumper stickers about dragons and science fiction, so I was confident the SMRC meeting was still going on. I let myself in the side door and went downstairs.

The walls of the stairway were still covered in heavy industrial plastic to hide the fire damage. Downstairs was even worse. Piles of scorched drywall, and plywood with heat-bubbled paint, were pulled off the walls and stacked in the corners. I was surprised that the SMRC was able to use the place so soon after the fire, but then I thought maybe they were volunteering as part of the clean-up crew.

I entered the large, open room in the basement. Most of the windows were covered with tarp, but a few of them let in a sooty light. The light seemed unreal, somehow, like it hadn't come from the normal sun but from some strange alien star where the laws of light worked differently.

A large knot of SMRC people stood in the center of the room. They were in a ragged oval, facing each other like participants in a twenty-way staring contest. None of them moved. I shuffled forward to get a better look and accidentally knocked over a can of spray paint. At the sound of the can bouncing and rolling, they all started moving at once. A few of them picked up boxes of charred items and carried them into another room, while others swept and mopped.

The change was instantaneous. They went from absolute stillness to busy, normal, everyday motion in the span of a eye-blink. It was incredibly creepy. I had to fight the urge to back away.

None of them paid attention to me at first, but then a woman stopped and noticed I was there. It was Brocelinde, known to the regular world as Nan Peters, the SMRC membership coordinator.

"Hello," she said. While she talked, she smiled brightly at a point in the air just to the left of my face. "I remember you. You were at our demo day. You were here with the redhead. Calvin was talking to you."

When she said the word "Calvin," several other people stopped what they were doing and drifted over to stand behind her. I recognized two of them from the group of Calvin's friends who had jumped me.

"Where is Calvin?" asked the first one.

"We need to find Calvin now," said the second. Unlike the others, these two looked right at me. Somehow, this made their flat, expressionless faces even more disturbing.

Brocelinde was still smiling and making reassuring noises to the empty space next to me. "Can't you tell us?" she asked. "Please, it's very important that we talk to Calvin."

The rest of the SMRC people had gathered around. I scanned their faces to see if any of them held some kind of human expression, but there was nothing. They all might as well have been sleepwalking.

Then I saw the piece of glass. There was a lumpy cardboard box in the corner, filled with half-burned garbage. A tall piece of broken plate glass was shoved in against one side. Its top was jagged, and it looked like a hideous accident just waiting to happen, the kind of thing they re-enact in safety training videos. The glass was angled in such a way that it reflected most of the room. I could see myself, and I looked fine, but everyone else seemed hazy, half-hidden behind human-shaped clouds of thin black mist.

I recognized the shapes of those clouds. My stomach tightened.

"It's very important that we find Calvin right away," Brocelinde repeated. "Can you tell us where he is?"

When I glanced back to her, *she* seemed hazy as well. It didn't last long enough for me to clearly see what was behind the image of the pleasant-looking middle-aged lady with the patchwork skirt, but that didn't matter. I knew already.

Knowing this gave me some kind of power. Or it made me stupid. Either one is possible, because the next thing I said was: "Don't bother. Calvin is somewhere where you're never going to find him. You can tell that to John Graze."

When Brocelinde and the rest of the crowd heard this, their humanity dropped away. I don't mean that I saw the creatures possessing them, but all the animation and movement drained away from their faces and bodies. They stopped being sleepwalkers and became mannequins made out of flesh.

They spoke at once, all of them, with one voice. "Tell Calvin: Run. Run as far as he can and he will be allowed to live out his natural life. If he remains, he will not."

The voices didn't quite sync up with the movements of their mouths. It was like a ventriloquist act, which is what I imagine it really was.

I backed up a step and shook my head. "Not good enough," I said. I sounded a lot braver than I actually felt, but all the frustrations and fears of the last few days were suddenly transformed into a strange energy. I wanted John Graze to hear me. "Your light shows, your little monsters, playing with people like they were Lego guys, it's just kind of sad. You won't get away with it."

I paused for a second, then added, "And Bob Daisley was a way better bass player than you."

I snapped a picture of the SMRC people with my Holga and ran up the stairs. Once I was a few stoplights away, I realized that the focus ring was dialed out to the "landscape" setting, so whatever had ended up on the film—either the SMRC people or the ghostly monsters inside—the image was probably nothing more than a dark blur on a dark background.

When I got to Macie's house, I was ready to tell her what I'd seen, but she stopped me dead before I could get two words out.

"William got arrested."

That floored me. All I could do was stand there on the doorstep, blinking at her while my mind raced to catch up. Eventually, she nudged me aside so she could join me on the porch and stop letting the air conditioning out.

"It happened in the middle of the night yesterday," she said. "I heard it from Micah. His brother knows William's brother."

"Micah called you?"

"He was letting people know about William. Calm down."

"I'm calm. Go ahead."

"William got in this huge fight with his parents last night. It started out about something stupid—like fingerprints on the butter or something."

"Fingerprints on the butter?"

"Yeah, I know. But can't you see William doing that? Anyway, the fight just got bigger and bigger—William said he hated his parents and his parents said if he couldn't live with their rules, he could live without a car, money, food, or a roof over his head."

"Wow."

"Yeah. Eventually they were just screaming at each other. Then, later that night when everybody else was asleep, William came downstairs and set the dining room on fire."

When William and I were in junior high, I had been in that dining room every other weekend, playing board games. I remembered its white carpet and carefully arranged crystal things and fake plants. He'd probably chosen the right room, I thought.

"When the fire alarms went off, his parents found William standing on the table, surrounded by fire. The firefighters had to tackle him to get him out of there. And when they put the fire out, they found all kinds of stuff on the table. William had emptied out his mom's medical bag and was mixing up a bunch of stuff: pills and serums and things. Nobody knows what he was trying to do."

"Is he still in jail?"

"I don't know. Micah didn't say. He wouldn't be, would he? His parents would get him out, don't you think?"

It was hard to say. William was the youngest of five kids, and I always got the feeling that his parents pretty much let them all sink or swim on their own. Besides, he'd just set their dining room on fire. I could imagine they'd want some time to cool off from that.

Macie squeezed my hand. "This is still just the beginning, Hal. A lot of people have those notebooks with the runes in them. Is something like that going to happen to all of them?"

"It might."

"How soon can Calvin's friends get him free?"

"Well…" I began.

By the time I'd explained to Macie that the SMRC people had all been taken by John Graze's creatures, I had to get to Jaya's. We made plans to meet up that evening at the Book Broker to break the news to Calvin that we were on our own.

13

I was afraid the Book Broker would be closed by the time I got there, but when I arrived, smelling of kimchee and industrial soap, there was a steady stream of people going in. They all carried long, narrow boxes and glanced furtively at each other, so for a minute I was concerned that we had run into yet another coven of oddballs. However, it turned out they were all there for a game tournament, and the boxes were filled with special playing cards. While the game players went upstairs, I found Macie in the used books catacomb and we let ourselves into the office.

"That's very, very bad," Calvin said when we told him what we'd learned over the course of the day. "If he's possessed all the SMRC-ers—" (he actually pronounced it 'smirkers') "—then he probably thinks he can use them for something. That means I must have been the only one he thought was too dangerous to keep alive. Hmm. When you think about it, that's kind of a compliment."

"What do we do now?" Macie sounded like she was in no mood to sit around and discuss things. She had good reason. Now that John Graze's runic time-bombs were starting to go off, she knew that things were going to get worse for her sister and most of her friends unless we did something about it.

Macie took a folded piece of paper out of her back pocket. It was the program from the summer musical. She had circled William's name in red, along with Sonia's and Lacey's. "There are a lot more names on here."

"Could you hold that up?" Calvin squinted up at the program, which must have been as big as a house to him. "Is that a picture of John Graze?"

"Yes."

"Tear it out. There's a lighter in the top drawer of my desk. Burn it."

Macie carefully tore the picture out and I reduced it to ashes without singeing my fingers, which I thought was quite an achievement.

"Images have power," Calvin said. "From now on, don't carry around anything that has his picture on it, or anything he's touched."

"You're kidding," Macie said.

"Remember those stories about primitive tribes that refused to have their pictures taken, because they thought it stole away a piece of their soul? Well, they're totally right."

I nodded. I don't think you can take very many pictures before you realize that's true.

"The image and the original have a link. Forever. That's Magic 101." Calvin sighed and lifted himself up from his doll-sized couch. "Consider that your first lesson. The first of many."

"You're teaching us more magic?" Macie asked.

"If John Graze has begun to make his move, then we don't have time to find someone else who knows how to get me out. By the time you find them, there may not be anything left to do. A couple dozen drama club kids can spread a lot of mayhem in a few weeks' time, and give Graze all the power he needs."

Calvin paced around inside his miniature room for a second. "Because of that, we're going to have to go with Plan B."

"You mean all this so far has been Plan A?" I asked.

Macie shushed me and Calvin continued. "Plan B is this: I'm going to teach you enough magic to get me out of here."

He threw himself back down on his couch and looked up at us. "The good news is that you did learn how to unseal the office door pretty quickly. So there's a decent chance that all this may work."

"I thought this was supposed to be dangerous. Isn't that what you said before?" Macie asked.

"Yes. It is. That's why you're going to practice before you actually do anything."

"Are you sure about this?" If the tables were turned and I was the one depending on Macie and myself to set me free without dematerializing me or whatever, I'm not sure I would have sounded as confident as Calvin did.

"I'm sure. Mostly. Right now, it's the best option we've got. Anyway, a lot of the stuff I told you earlier was sort of exaggerated. This'll be fine."

"Really?"

"Trust me."

Under Calvin's direction, we gathered up the papers scattered around the office and started to put them in order. When arranged correctly, they formed a sort of textbook on magic. That was what Calvin told us, anyway. Apparently, it was every wizard's duty (he cringed whenever I called him a "warlock") to write up all that he had learned, and all the details of his personal magical system, so it could be passed on to the next generation. Sadly, the reality was that Calvin hadn't got much further than a rough draft.

"It'll be good enough to start with," he assured us. "There are places where there's not enough detail, and there are places that are just wrong, but I'll be here to talk you through it."

There were no page numbers on anything, of course, but Macie seemed to have a good eye for how it all fit together. I leafed through a few of the pages as she stacked them up. The first thing Calvin was going to have to talk us through was the handwriting. The pages that were in code were bad enough, but even the stuff that claimed to be plain English appeared to have been written in the midst of an epileptic fit.

"Just start with the introduction. It should give you an idea of what you'll need to do to make the spells work. Don't worry if it sounds intimidating—you won't have to learn all the stuff I talk about, just enough to help me get out of here. I've been doing some thinking, and I'm pretty sure that if you can get me halfway there, I can do the rest from inside. So this will be even easier."

I let Macie take the pages home because she was able to make more sense out of Calvin's cardiogram handwriting than I could. Also, she was the one who had made the door-opening spell work the last time. If we had to use quick-and-dirty, jury-rigged magic to get Calvin out of his box, we might as well go with the person who seemed to have some talent for it.

When I got home I took all of my Left Hand Ritual CDs and cassettes, as well as the couple of vinyl albums I'd picked up at a thrift store but never got around to finding a turntable for, and hid them in a box in the basement. I suppose I should have thrown them away or set them on fire in the driveway like some over-enthusiastic backwoods preacher, but I couldn't. Evil wizardry or not, they were still my old friends. I just hoped that John Graze's magical reach didn't extend to the digital files I'd ripped onto my computer.

The next day at work, I straightened the tables and got ready to open while Nate prepped for lunch. Jaya wasn't there yet. She had just bought the storefront next door, and was in the process of remodeling it into an extended dining room for the restaurant, so she sometimes left us to run things while she was busy intimidating contractors. I had just turned over the open/closed sign at eleven and was refilling the napkin holders on the back tables when the door-chimes rang and a customer came in.

It was Micah Tomey.

"Hey, Hal! Do you work here? I didn't know that."

"Yeah, this is my aunt's place."

"Your aunt's Korean?"

"That's what she keeps telling everyone."

All this got me was a blank look, which was about what it deserved. "I'm kidding," I said. "What can I get for you?"

He scanned the menu for a second. Then he looked up and stared at me for a good long time, like there was an extra page of the menu printed on my forehead. He shook his head and blinked. "Can I have the chicken special and a Coke?"

He gave me an odd smile, and I suddenly felt like he was making fun of me, like there was some kind of joke going on that he knew I wouldn't get.

After I ran the order back to Nate, Micah waved me over again. "Did you hear about William?" he asked. After I said I did, he added, "I figured Macie would tell you about it. You know, I had a feeling that he was going to lose it eventually." He looked up at me. "Oh, sorry. He was a friend of yours, wasn't he?"

There was that smile again.

"Yeah." I tried to keep my voice neutral. Even though Micah was better looking, and a better actor, and undoubtedly interested in my girlfriend, he was still a customer. "Is there anything else you need?"

Micah held up his fork. "Can I get another one? This one's got something on it."

I replaced his silverware while he kept smiling that weird smile at me, then I went back to checking the napkin holders. And I checked the hell out of them, too. There wasn't a napkin holder on the premises that didn't have the perfect number of napkins in it by the time I was through. Except for Micah's. That napkin holder could rot in hell for all I cared, but I tried not to show it, since I was a professional.

I brought Micah his chicken, and he ate it while staring into space. A couple of other customers had come in by that time, so I had something else to do besides glare at the back of his head. I was glad for the distraction. My mind kept drifting back to the industrial-sized woks we keep in the kitchen. I wondered what it would sound like if I bashed Micah in the head with one of those.

Micah brought up his check and I went around the counter to the register. As I rang it up, he said, "How's Macie?"

I didn't look at him. "Good. She's starting up a summer class." I wasn't going to mention what she had begun studying.

As I handed him back his change, his fingers closed around mine. He leaned in. "Hey, does she still wear those bras with the orange flowers on them?"

I pulled my hand back and stared. Did I just hear that?

Micah kept talking. "God, you have to be a damn locksmith just to get them off. Of course, that didn't bother you, did it? You'd just rip 'em in half."

I tried to say something, but my mouth just opened and closed like a goldfish.

"She told me all about that. She tells me all kinds of things. We're great friends. She said it was weird at first, but thinking about it kind of got her hot. So, thanks for that."

I felt like I'd been turned inside out. Despite the clouds of steam rolling in from the kitchen, I was cold. I wanted to yell at him, tell him he was lying, insist that Macie would never do that, but I knew that anything I tried to say would come out like the protests of a whiny twelve-year old. My fingers tingled and my vision went weird. I watched a photo negative of Micah give me that knowing smirk one more time and leave the restaurant. I stood there leaning against the counter for either five seconds or a day and a half, then I lurched toward the kitchen and called to Nate.

"I've gotta go for a minute. Can you watch the front?"

"No, I can't—"

"Nate, please?"

"I don't even remember how to work the register!"

"I'll be right back, I promise." I would have promised anything at that point, and forgotten all about it an instant later. As soon as I got the vaguest of nods from Nate, I was gone.

Outside, I saw Micah half a block away. He was looking at the guitars in the windows of the pawn shop. I wasn't even sure why I was following him, but I couldn't let him go. I wasn't going to fight him, and if I tried to get him to take back what he had said, he was just going to laugh at me, but at that moment I knew that if I let him go it would be the most terrible thing in the world.

Micah turned and unlocked his car. I was parked in the lot across the street and by the time I reached my car, Micah had pulled away and was slowly driving down Third Street.

I'd never tailed another car, the way they do in spy movies, but I managed to keep Micah in sight. I probably had an easier time than most spies, since I didn't care at all whether Micah knew he was being followed. It still wasn't easy, and I had to run a couple of red lights and cut off a few cars, but I stayed with him. There was a quiet, reasonable voice in my head that suggested I'd be better off stopping this craziness before I got pulled over and had to explain it all to a cop. Not only that, the voice said, but I also had no idea what I was supposed to do when Micah eventually got to wherever he was going. I told myself to shut up. I would figure out what to do when the time came. I rubbed my shoulder, which had suddenly begun to hurt again.

We were on the Lloyd Expressway, heading east out of town, past the strip malls and the new hospital, then into Newburgh. I knew that Micah didn't live around here. He lived on the north side of town. I had been to his parties. I had seen his house. When he got off the highway, I realized that we both knew someone who did live around here: John Graze.

Micah drove past the rows of mansions with their fenced-in yards, the same road I'd driven down when I first delivered bulgogi beef and fried eggplant to John Graze's house. He got ahead of me at a four-way stop, where an old lady in a Cadillac got the jump on me and ended up between us. I saw Micah turn into John Graze's driveway and I followed along as soon as I got there. The gate was open. As I passed, I noticed that the little black speaker grille on the post by the gate had been smashed in.

Micah had parked around the back, next to the wing of the house that contained John Graze's nest. I got out of my car and stared at him. I didn't know what I wanted from him, but I knew I wanted *something*. I wanted him to tell me that what he'd said wasn't true, but deep down I knew that even if he did, I wouldn't believe him. It *felt* true, even if it wasn't, and I didn't know what I could do to change that.

Micah leaned on his car door as I walked, stiff-legged, up to him. "How's it going, Hal? I thought that was you following me. What's up?"

I picked up a broken tree branch, as long as my arm and as thick as a baseball bat, a piece of debris from the recent storm.

"I swear, I thought you knew," Micah said. His hands were up and he was laughing, like I was threatening him with a water balloon. "She hooks up with a new guy every show. Some kind of actress thing. I don't think she can help it. She really didn't tell you?"

I took another step forward.

"I guess not. Look, it's not a big deal, right? It's not like you love her or anything. She's just a—"

I'd never hit anyone before, let alone clubbed anyone with a tree branch. As it turns out, it's not hard. I mean, once you get that little nudge to push you out of the restrictive straitjacket of civilized human behavior, it feels pretty natural. The only real surprise was how much it hurt my hands. It felt like hitting a fence post. Micah dropped like a sack of potatoes. I hit him two more times, with the pain vibrating from my hands to my shoulder, then I realized something was wrong.

Micah was lying on his side with his eyes open and the same smug smile on his face. He wasn't even looking at me, but he kept laughing a soft little laugh, like a talking doll with some broken mechanism inside. My first impulse was to hit him in the face with the branch, to smash that stupid grin and shut up that laugh. I almost did, too. I was holding the branch over my head, ready to swing, when I hesitated. My hands started to shake, and the branch fell out of my grip.

I took a step backward. All of a sudden, I felt cold. What the hell was the matter with me? What was I doing? This wasn't me. This wasn't about Macie, and this wasn't about Micah. This was insanity. I took a deep breath. My shoulder still ached, right where John Graze's creature had bitten me.

Then I heard the noises. It was a clattering sound, a clicking, scratching, buzzing sound that could almost have been a gust of wind rustling through the trees that surrounded us, but wasn't. I couldn't see anyone or anything up there, but I knew I wasn't alone. I got the feeling they were disappointed that I hadn't bashed Micah's skull in, which must have been the whole reason for luring me here.

I crept away from the trees and toward the house. I wanted to get away from whatever was lurking in the trees, but I also wanted to see if John Graze was watching me from the window, hip-deep in the disgusting filth of his nest. I wanted to see him. I wanted to let him know that he still hadn't gotten me, that I still wasn't under his control. I knew this wasn't too smart, but I had been doing a lot of stupid stuff recently, and I was starting to get used to it.

I didn't see John Graze when I looked into the window. I didn't see his nest, either. I didn't see anything in there, just a big empty room with French doors leading to the swimming pool beyond. A few days ago, this room had been full, and the walls had been covered with writing. Now, everything was gone, as empty as if he had moved out years ago.

I blinked my eyes, then froze. Something wasn't right. For a split second, I hadn't seen the empty room. I hadn't seen the filthy nest, either. I had seen a burned-out shell. In that instant, while my eyes weren't completely open or completely closed, I saw charred floors, and blackened wallpaper that peeled off the walls to reveal scorched plaster and crumbling beams. My hand was resting on the windowsill. When I rubbed my fingers together, they felt gritty, though I couldn't see anything on them.

I backed up. I felt like I couldn't trust my own eyes, which was incredibly disorienting. If I'd had Calvin's charm thing with me, I might have seen what everything really looked like, but it didn't matter too much. I knew. On the ground, Micah hadn't moved, and was still laughing in that weird mechanical way. My eyes swum and he sort of flickered, the way the house had, and I caught a glimpse of the beetle-skinned thing that controlled him. I looked away, then realized that the trees above us had a few shadows that shouldn't have been there. I edged back to my car. As I got in, I heard a high-pitched laugh from somewhere, and thought about the blonde girl-thing that had been lurking outside Calvin's apartment.

Once I was safely on the highway, I called Macie. There was no response, not even a voicemail prompt, so I called her house.

"Hello, Hal. How are you?" It was Macie's mom.

"I'm doing all right, Mrs. Hart. Is Macie there?"

Silence. "Hello?" I said, concerned that dark forces may have sabotaged my phone.

"She told me she was with you."

"Oh. Well…" I trailed off for a second. There was very little you could say in this situation that didn't make things worse. "If I see her, should I have her call you?"

"Yes, please."

I drove on. If Micah hadn't warped my judgment—which he definitely had not—if he hadn't found my weak spot and attacked it mercilessly—which he absolutely hadn't—I would have found my mind drifting to all the places Macie could possibly be while she told her parents she was with me. Like, for example, with Marcus Wallace, who had been in the bohemian chorus, and went to our high school. Or Carlos, whom she had dated before (and a little bit during) the time when we first got together. I always had the impression that Carlos deserved to be with Macie more than I did. He was taller, played baseball, and had that soulful look that girls seemed to love. He was serious. He was going to be somebody. Me, I liked plays and old junk. I could tell jokes, and I knew how to make her look good on film. I always suspected this wasn't enough, and felt like she'd come to the same conclusion eventually, too.

Stop it, I told myself. Stop thinking about it. Stop thinking at all. I reached under my seat and slammed one of my garage-sale tapes into the player. Left Hand Ritual. Of course it was. I hadn't checked the tapes in my car when I'd cleaned out the rest of my stuff. I didn't change the tape, though. If you really wanted to stop thinking, there wasn't anything better.

My hands were shaking as I pressed the rewind button. I tried to take a deep breath but couldn't manage it. I reminded myself that this was all part of John Graze's magic. These weren't my real thoughts. Like everyone else, I was being manipulated to produce craziness and emotional chaos.

That helped to clear the mental clouds a little. And then I had a pretty good idea of where to find Macie.

When I got to the Book Broker, I sat in the parking lot for a minute, partially to make sure I'd calmed down sufficiently, but also to finish listening to the song that was playing. It was "Overlord," my second favorite track from the *Black Aura* album. I was a little surprised I could still listen to Left Hand Ritual without freaking out, but I could. It was going to take more than what had happened already to make me give up my favorite band. I reached under my seat and grabbed the folder of photos from John Graze's house.

When I went inside, there was a guy with a ponytail and wire-frame glasses behind the counter. He nodded at me. "She's in the back," he said.

"Thanks." I guess it hadn't taken long for us to become regulars here. I couldn't decide if that was a good thing or a bad thing.

In the office, Macie was sitting on the couch concentrating on the sheaf of papers in her hand. Calvin's box was open on the desk beside her, and if you didn't know there was a tiny dude in there, it looked like she was studying for a test just like any normal person.

"Hi," she said, once she noticed I was there.

"Come here." When she stood up I hugged her as tightly as I could, one of those long hugs where you try to memorize the contours of the other person's body against your own.

"Are you okay?" she asked at last.

"Yeah. Just needed that. I missed you."

I considered asking her, in some indirect way, about what I'd heard from Micah. But I didn't. That poison was meant for me, not her. It was up to me to believe it or not. I decided to let it drop.

"Is that Hal?" said the voice from the box. "Hello, Hal! Did you bring the pictures?"

"I called your house," I said to Macie.

She winced. "Oh, no."

"Yeah."

"I'll have to tell them I was at the library. Do you think they'll believe that you got called in to work and I spent the afternoon reading?"

"That depends. Have they ever watched television before?"

"I'll work on it." She picked up the stack of papers from the couch. "Right now, though, watch this."

She squinted at the desk, made a face that was so serious it was adorable, then mumbled some words under her breath. A metal globe the size of a softball, with the patterns of the constellations engraved on it, levitated half a foot off the surface of the desk and drifted over to the opposite side, then nestled back among the papers.

"Wow."

"Yeah." Macie's eyes were shining the way they did when she got offstage after a play. She seemed charged with some kind of electricity I'd never seen in her before.

"You just learned that?" I asked.

"Most of it. I started last night and Calvin taught me the rest."

"She's the best student I've ever seen," said the voice from the box. "If she keeps this up, she'll be able to get me out of this a lot faster than I thought."

"That's awesome. Congratulations." I meant it, but I couldn't help feeling a little creeped out, too. It was great for her to be good at something, but when her new hobby involved things like reversing gravity, teleportation, and probably turning the moon to blood, it was... Well, it was just weird.

I slid over to Calvin's box and showed him the folder. "Here they are," I said. I took out the prints and held them up over the box. "Sorry they're so big. I guess I should have brought you a contact print. At least then you would have been able to get a closer look at them."

"It's all right. I don't think I would have been able to take them from you. There's something in the nature of this box that prevents things from passing through. That's what Macie's going to do when she's ready—stretch that barrier far enough that I should be able to push through on my own."

Following Calvin's instructions, I propped up some of the photos against the pencil holders and empty tea tins on the desk, then scooted them close to the box so that Calvin could look at them the way you might stare up at a billboard—not a lot of detail, but enough to get the general idea.

Macie picked up one of the pictures and studied it. She ran her finger along the patterns, as if she understood some of them.

"This was in his house?"

"Yep. Surprisingly, it wasn't one of the rooms they showed when *Kerrang* magazine did a tour in 1986."

Macie examined the rest of the pictures, one by one. "Some of this stuff is pretty primitive compared to what you're showing me, Calvin," she said.

"Don't be fooled. Primitive can still be dangerous. If someone kills you with a rock, you're just as dead as if they used an F-16."

"Still, though. If this is the best he can do…"

"It may not even be there anymore," I interrupted. I explained that I had been out to his house again today, and described how I had seen it flickering between its normal appearance and the burned ruins. I studiously left out any mention of why I had ended up there in the first place. Luckily for me, they forgot to ask.

I pointed to the wrapped packet that Macie still had hanging around her neck. "If I'd had that, I think I could have seen what was really there. Though I'm pretty sure it would have been even freakier."

"Assuming what you saw was true," said the voice from the box, "he's completed the preliminary stages of his plan. He doesn't need his home base or his safe nest anymore, so he put a match to it. The illusion is just there to keep the neighbors fooled."

"Why would he burn down his own house?" Macie asked.

"When a wizard is dealing with powers outside of himself, sometimes it's necessary for him to demonstrate that he's totally committed to his magical working. It gives him and his creatures a stronger bond. The ritual is all he's got now. There's no way back for him."

"So what does that mean?" I asked.

"It means you two have to get those spells learned as soon as possible. I need to get out of here."

14

Macie called me later that night, while I was watching TV and taking apart my Diana camera to figure out what was causing the shutter to stick.

"Hey, what'cha doing?" I asked.

"Homework. I needed a break, so I wanted somebody fun to talk to. Can you be fun?"

"I can be hilarious. Is this homework from Calvin?"

"Yeah. It's making my head spin a little bit. I think I'm working too fast, but I can't stand sitting around and not being able to do anything until Calvin is free."

"Do you want me to take over for a while?" I asked.

"That's okay. It's not that bad. It's almost…"

"What?"

"No, it's stupid. Forget it."

"Tell me. Stupid's never stopped us before."

"Okay. It's almost like I already knew this stuff and I'm just going back over my old notes to remind myself."

I didn't say anything to that. I was glad she couldn't see me shiver over the phone.

"See, it's stupid," Macie said.

"No. No. I totally get it. I felt the same when I got my first rangefinder camera. Like it had been waiting for me."

"Shut up."

"Seriously, though. That's great. It's great that one of us can do it. Calvin needs it. *We* need it." I tried to keep a positive tone in my voice. It really was great that she could do this, but in another way it was also *kind of* great. As much as I said out loud that I was happy my girlfriend could break the laws of nature with an instinctive ease, it was still pretty damn strange. Like one of us had suddenly become less human.

"My sister's downstairs," Macie said, changing the subject.

"Is she, you know, okay?"

"Yeah, I think so. She's watching *Dune* for like the thirtieth time." Sandra had some non-mainstream tastes in movies, which had only gotten more pronounced following her bump on the head and subsequent demonic possession.

"Did you get in trouble with your parents when you got back? Again, I'm really sorry I screwed that up."

"No problem. They were just about on the way out when I got home, so they believed whatever I told them. I think they wanted to."

"Oh, yeah. This was their vacation, wasn't it?" Man, if there was one thing that symbolized how far I'd slipped into the insanity of the past few weeks, it's that I forgot when Macie's parents were going out of town. Her dad was heading to an insurance conference in Myrtle Beach, and her mom was tagging along. This was going to leave Macie under the nominal supervision of her sister Sandra, whom we had suspected would be a whole lot less interested in the tiny details of who was where, when, and for how long. I had made more than a few mental plans for those four days, and now the whole thing was an afterthought. Realizing that made me a little sad, and a whole lot angry.

"So you're making progress with Calvin's stuff?" I asked her, just to keep the conversation going.

"Yeah. It makes me nervous, though, when I think about doing it for real. Hey—I think I just figured something out. Is it okay if I hang up? I want to check this before I lose it."

I wished her luck and went back to my camera parts, my WD-40 pen, and my growing case of nerves.

A little later, I switched off the TV and went to bed. Generally I'm the kind of person who likes to stay up late, but I was exhausted. Having a regular job this summer had kept me from developing the 2am-10am sleep cycle that always made the first week of school so miserable. This was useful because when my phone rang at one o'clock that morning, I'd at least had a couple hours of sleep to help me deal with what came next.

I was staggering across the room to get my phone before I'd even fully awakened from my dream. "Hello?" I said, with a tongue that still felt like it belonged to someone else.

"Hal?" That woke me up. It was Macie's voice. She was frightened and upset, and it hit me like a glass of water in the face.

"What's the matter?"

"It's Sandra. Hal, can you come over right now?"

"Yeah. Sure." I was wide awake. "Let me get some pants on. I'll be right over."

"Hal, hurry. Please."

As I got dressed, I thought about what this was all going to mean. My parents hated me sneaking out in the middle of the night. The last time I'd really gotten yelled at was when I'd gone out to meet some girl who had been working the graveyard shift at Wesselman's supermarket. But there was nothing I could do about that right now. My real concern was that they might wake up and catch me before I got out of the house. I crept downstairs with my shoes in my hand and stopped at the kitchen table to write a note: "I'm sorry I had to sneak out, but it was an emergency. I'll explain when I get back."

I left the note, with that optimistic last sentence, on the counter. If they happened to wake up when I drove off, which they might, since their bedroom window faced the driveway, I hoped the note would forestall them from freaking out completely and calling the police. Although, given the rate of insanity among my circle of friends right now, I wouldn't say the chances were too good.

The house disappeared behind me, but I didn't feel any better. As anyone woken up in the middle of the night by a frightened voice on the phone might be, I was anxious. I reached into my box of tapes and shoved one into the deck without looking. It was Left Hand Ritual. No surprise there. If I had picked some other band from the Eighties to be a fan of—Bon Jovi, say—would I be in this situation right now?

It was a bootleg live recording, and after a minute I recognized which one it was. It was the Kansas City bootleg, which I'd gotten a couple of years ago from an older cousin, who had found it while cleaning out his garage. It was the last concert with all the original members—the last complete concert, anyway. The next stop on the tour, Minneapolis, had been where the band imploded for good. The Minneapolis show was where Tommy Jason, the guitar player, had actually thrown a chair at John in the middle of the performance. That, of course, led to a fistfight on stage, refunds for the audience, and a two-month break in the tour while the rest of the band tried out new singers and bass players to replace

John. There was a legend that the sound man had actually recorded the Minneapolis show as well, and that there existed, somewhere in his personal archive, a tape of Left Hand Ritual trying to kill each other in front of fifteen thousand fans.

The Kansas City tape was a good one, by the standards of old bootlegs, which meant that the sound quality wasn't bad enough to give you a headache. I tried not to think too much about who was singing those songs and instead just listened to them as old favorites that I'd loved for years. They helped to take my mind off what I might be getting into.

When I arrived at Macie's house, the lights were on and there were no ambulances in the driveway. These seemed like positive signs. I parked on the street and got out of the car. I was nearly at the porch when the window to Macie's room flew open and I saw her lean out.

"Hal!" Upscale housing developments tend to be pretty quiet after midnight, so her shout sounded deafeningly loud. "Be careful!"

Before I could shout back, the front door opened. It was a faceless shape, silhouetted in the doorframe, but I could tell it was Sandra. I flinched, but only a little.

"Hi, Hal," Sandra said.

I walked up to the porch. "Sandra, what's going on?"

"Nothing's going on."

"What about Macie?"

"Macie's not here." Sandra's shirt had a huge dark stain on one side, starting at the ribs and running all the way down. Her eyes weren't focused quite right, either. It was like she was looking at something on the horizon instead of right in front of her.

"Goodbye, Hal. I'll tell her you stopped by." Like a bad animatronic device, she turned awkwardly and took a heavy step back into the house. As she turned, I saw a hammer tucked into her belt. The head was wet with some glistening liquid. She closed the door and I heard the lock turn.

My heart raced. What was I supposed to do now? I was in the shadow of the porch and couldn't see Macie's window anymore. Should I run back and ask her if the garage door was open?

Then I heard the crash. It was like someone had dumped a drawer of silverware onto the floor. I thought I heard someone scream, too.

At this point, I probably wasn't thinking very clearly. I looked around wildly and my eyes fell on the garden gnome, sitting placidly next to a bush full of pink flowers, with a tiny shovel over its shoulder. That gnome, which had been there ever since I'd known Macie, alternated between cute and ridiculous every time I saw it.

But now, though, things were different. I had a job for it. I picked the gnome up. It was a heavy little thing, solid concrete instead of plaster. I hesitated. I'd like to say that this was one last flash of good judgment causing me to reconsider my course of action, but it wasn't. I was just adjusting my grip. I held onto its pointed red hat like a handle, swung it back and forth a couple of times, then hurled it through the Harts' front window.

A minute ago, I thought Macie shouting in the middle of the night had sounded loud. As it turns out, that was nothing compared to a big pane of plate glass shattering into a zillion pieces. I didn't stop to think about it. I kicked a few stray shards out of the window frame and climbed inside.

At the other end of the house, I saw Sandra's shadow moving against the kitchen wall. I grabbed the gnome and ran upstairs.

Macie's door was closed. There were deep gouges in the wood and splintery cracks in the doorframe right where the doorknob and lock mechanism connected. I pounded on the door.

"Macie! It's me!" I looked over my shoulder. Sandra was nowhere in sight. Yet. "Let me in!"

The door opened a crack. When she saw it was me, she grabbed me by the shirt and pulled me inside, slamming the door behind us and shoving her desk chair under the knob.

"We have to get out of here," she gasped.

"I had a feeling about that. What the hell's going on?"

She shook her head. "Later."

Macie was wearing a big blue t-shirt and a thin pair of shorts with lace trim along the edges. *So this was what she slept in,* I thought to myself. I had always been curious.

On the bed behind her, there was a scattered pile of laundry. On top, I saw the underwear with the orange flowers that Micah had mentioned. Had that been a lucky guess on his part, magical telepathy, or something else?

Macie interrupted my thoughts. "Where's Sandra?" she asked.

"Downstairs. If we hurry, we can—"

The door rattled with a heavy crash. It actually gave an inch or two before the chair stopped it. Macie choked off a shriek and I nearly bit my tongue.

"Macie, open the door," said the voice from the other side. "I just want to talk."

This was the point where I realized I should have stayed outside and helped Macie escape, rather than running inside and getting trapped along with her, but you know what they say about hindsight.

Macie pointed. "The window."

"Really?" This was not a small jump, and I felt my crazy bravado starting to waver.

The door shook again. This time it opened wide enough for Sandra's hand to reach through and grope for the chair that blocked her way. I bashed it closed again, using the gnome as a battering ram.

"The window," I said.

For split second, I was hung up on a point of chivalry. In a situation like this, was it better manners to let the lady go through the window first, while I held the line of defense? Or should *I* go through the window first and find out whether the fall was fatal before Macie tried it?

This was a thorny problem, but Macie solved it by slithering over the windowsill and dropping to the lawn with a thump.

The door rattled ominously, then creaked as if something was being driven into the wood. It was time to go. As I ran for the window, something caught my eye among the brushes and bottles and girl junk on top of Macie's dresser. It was a tiny packet of paper wrapped up with yellow thread, looped over the upraised arms of a figure on a gold-toned trophy. It was Calvin's charm. I shoved it in my pocket.

Through the window, I could see that Macie had cleared the landing area and was crouched by the nose of my car. I tossed the gnome first—I felt like the gnome and I were friends now—then swung my legs over the sill. I turned around and hung by my hands, to shorten the distance to the ground. I forced myself to let go and fell in a heap onto the lawn. I tripped over my own feet and half-stumbled the rest of the way to the curb.

Once we were in the car, I dug my keys out of my pocket and had to untangle them from the little paper charm and its cord. I dropped the charm in the cup holder and put the key in the ignition. There was an agonizing half-second where I was certain the car wasn't going to start. But the engine turned over eventually and we were gone by the time Sandra returned to the porch. I don't know if she tried to follow us or not. I didn't look in the rear-view mirror. I didn't want to know.

We didn't say anything until we were clear of Macie's development. When we got to the highway, she seemed to relax a little and slumped into the seat.

"God, Hal. Thank you," she said at last.

"What happened?"

Macie didn't answer right away. I could tell she was looking for the right words.

"I was getting ready for bed. I said goodnight to Sandra. She didn't say anything back, but that was normal. She does that all the time now. I didn't think anything about it, so I just went to bed. I don't remember how long I was asleep, but I heard Sandra making noise in the kitchen. Crashes and rattles, like she was digging around in the drawer for something. Then it got quiet. I can't tell you why, but the quiet was what scared me. I got out of bed and listened. Pretty soon, I could hear her coming up the stairs, so I locked the door. Sandra's been into mean practical jokes ever since she got hurt, but this seemed different. I didn't know what to do. I heard her footsteps in the hall outside my room, then nothing. It felt like forever, then she shook the doorknob. Then another minute of nothing. That was the worst part: the waiting. Then she spoke to me. She said, 'Come out, Macie. I need you.' But it wasn't her voice. I don't know how else to say it—it was her voice, but it wasn't *her*. I just kept quiet. I guess I hoped she would go away. She didn't. A little bit later, the whole door shook like she had thrown herself against it. After that, I heard a scraping sound, like she was dragging something sharp down the length of the door. I was so scared I couldn't think straight. I knew she was going to try again, but I kept hoping and hoping she'd go away. It all started up again: the doorknob, that horrible voice—the exact same words the exact same way, like a tape recording. That's when I was able to make myself run across the room and call you. And she kept doing the exact same things, over and over, until you got there."

I didn't know what to say. I'd been terrified out of my wits just listening to that story as we drove through the dark. I was amazed Macie had been able to live through it with her sanity intact. I reached out and held her hand, which was the best thing I could think to do.

"Hal?" she asked.

"Yeah?"

Macie looked down at my feet. "Is that my parents' gnome?"

I nodded. "Yes." There wasn't much else I could say about that.

We were getting out of the suburbs and closer to the city. I had been driving on autopilot as I listened, and must have automatically headed for the brighter lights.

"Is there someplace I can take you? I mean, is there somebody you want…"

She shook her head like she was trying to shoo away a gnat. "I don't know. I just don't know. I can't think." I noticed that her bare legs had broken out in goosebumps. I turned off the air conditioner. We were stopped at a red light. On one side was the strip mall with the camera store where I bought my film. Around the corner in the other direction was the gigantic multiplex movie theater where Macie and I would buy tickets for unpopular movies and make out in the back row. The light turned green. I pulled into the strip mall and made a U-turn in the parking lot. I got back on the highway and drove off in the opposite direction, back the way we'd come.

When we got back to my house, all the lights were still off. I shut off my headlights before I turned and coasted into the driveway. I was lucky not to plow over the mailbox, which has been the source of more than one close call, even in full visibility.

Once we stopped, I looked down at her bare feet, which were tucked up under her. "The driveway's all gravel. Do you want me to carry you?"

"Are you kidding?"

"I'm capable of carrying you," I said.

"It's okay. I'll be fine."

We tiptoed to the porch and I let us in the back door, which I'd left unlocked. Once inside, I put my finger to my lips in a totally unnecessary "shh" gesture and took her hand to lead her upstairs to my room. As I eased the door shut, it seemed that my room was much closer to my parents' room than it ever had been in the past.

"Is this okay?" she whispered as she sat down on my bed.

"I guess so." I nodded. "Yeah. It is." It would have to be. My parents would go ballistic, as parents do, if they found out about this tomorrow, but what other choices were there at half past two in the morning?

"I'm worried, Hal."

I put my keys on the dresser and sat next to her on the bed. "It's okay. My dad'll go to work in the morning and my mom usually has errands to run. We'll sneak out after they leave."

"Not that. My sister."

"Oh."

"It's just going to get worse, Hal. We can't let him keep doing this. Everyone from the play, they're all going to end up like that. And they're going to spread it to anyone else they get close to. It'll keep growing until we stop him."

"We'll stop him. We will. I promise." We kissed. One of those long, almost violent kisses, where we clung to each other like we were afraid of what we would have to see if we ever let go. I don't remember how, but soon we were stretched out on the bed. My hands were under her shirt, under the thin elastic of her shorts. She was struggling with the button on my jeans when I saw she was still shivering.

I pushed myself up until I was sitting again. "Wait," I whispered. "We shouldn't."

"What?" She sounded dazed.

"This isn't right."

She blinked at me heavily, like she wasn't sure what language I was speaking. As much as I wanted to, and I really, really, did want to, she was still shell-shocked and not thinking clearly. I didn't want it to be like that. She didn't say anything, and I was glad, because I didn't think I could find the right words to explain it. Instead, I just pulled the sheets up to her shoulders and kissed her again.

"You sleep," I said. "I'll be here."

I sat on the edge of the bed and watched her for a while. Within a minute she was breathing regularly and I knew she was asleep. I was exhausted, too, but my eyes didn't want to close. So I kept watching her sleep. I wanted to reach out and run my hand over her hip, but I told myself not to. Instead, I stood up and picked out one of my cameras. What film was in it? Black and white 400? That would work, if I was careful. I did a quick check with the light meter and took a couple of pictures of her sleeping. She looked so beautiful and so peaceful. I hoped she wouldn't be too upset if I ever showed them to her. I stretched. Still not tired. I didn't think it would be a good idea to stay here and keep meditating on the girl in my bed, so I crept downstairs to get something to drink.

I didn't turn on any lights until I got to the kitchen, and even then it was just the little lamp over the sink. If my parents hadn't woken up by this point, they probably weren't going to, but I didn't want to take any chances. I got a glass from the cupboard, threw away the note I had left on the counter, and went to the fridge to pour myself some milk. I was walking back to the counter to drink it when my bare foot skidded on something. At first I thought it was a magazine that had fallen off of the table—it felt slippery and glossy underfoot. But the shape was wrong. I bent down to get a better look in the gloom.

It was an album sleeve. When I picked it up, I saw that it was *Black Aura*, the third Left Hand Ritual album. My favorite one. I set my glass down. All of a sudden, I felt very cold. I didn't have this album on vinyl. This wasn't mine.

Then I felt a hand on my shoulder.

John Graze stood behind me. In the dim light he seemed to waver, as if he wasn't completely solid. In fact, he looked like a multiple exposure photograph. That's the best way I can describe what I saw when I looked at him. I could see the John Graze of the early Left Hand Ritual albums: all Eighties hair and motorcycle leather, then the

John Graze of today: short gray hair, clothes like anybody else, and at the same time there was the John Graze I saw when I listened to the music: dark and godlike and heroic—the guy I always wanted to be in my daydreams, the guy I felt like when I was on stage acting in a play. In addition to all that, there was another version that I could just barely see. There weren't any details, but I could tell it was something rotten and angry.

He held out his hand and the copy of *Black Aura* materialized in it.

"This was the best one," he said. "The one where we did everything right."

I didn't say anything. I couldn't. If I could have gotten to the silverware drawer I would have threatened him with a cheese grater or something, but I couldn't move.

"We toured on that album forever. Thousands of people would scream for every gesture, every note I played." He looked down at me. He seemed to have gotten taller. "I thought that was it. I thought that was as good as it got. When it went away, I thought I was going to die. Then I discovered the truth. The power on a stage is just an illusion. But there was a way to go beyond it. To become more than the master of an audience. To become the master of reality."

He tilted his head to one side and I followed his eyes. On the kitchen counter, a line of runes wrote themselves in letters of fire. The flames lit his face from underneath and made it look like a human-shaped mask over something far more terrifying.

"You children, so full of life. All that energy. It flows from you to my creatures. It feeds them, lets them grow and multiply. They will remake the world in my image. This world's laws will be my laws."

He held his hand over my head, almost like a priest blessing someone. "And you will watch. Your friends, your family, your girl. They will all belong to me. And you will see what they become."

Suddenly John Graze became normal-sized again. We were almost eye-to-eye. "But it doesn't have to happen. You can save them, if you want. Whatever I might do, I can guarantee they will be safe forever. Do you want that?"

I nodded. God help me, I nodded.

"Find the wizard. You know who I mean. The one who was in my house. I know he's somewhere, but I can't find him. You can, though. Find him and destroy him. Destroy him and they'll all be safe."

The burning runes cast shadows on the wall that flickered and jumped. In my mind's eye, I could see those shadows glowing brightly, turning into real flames that climbed the walls and consumed the house. Then I could see faces in the shadows. The faces of Macie and my parents. My aunt Jaya and Nate the cook. The faces grew darker, replaced by the insect-skinned, bug-eyed creatures that now lived inside Macie's sister and most of my friends.

"It doesn't have to happen." I heard John's voice while I stared fixedly at the shadows. "You can keep it from happening. Just destroy the magician."

I blinked hard to keep from crying. I was struggling for air. Up until now, and I really hate to admit it, but this whole adventure hadn't seemed completely real. It was something I could leave at the Book Broker or at Macie's house and go home, where I could relax and develop my pictures and not worry too much. But now, here it was. In my kitchen. Its hands were around my throat. All I could think about was getting it away from me. And it had offered me a way.

The runes died away to nothing but a faint glow, and within a couple of seconds they were gone completely. John Graze, or the apparition of him, was gone, too. But I could still feel his presence, like the way you know someone else is in the house even if you can't see or hear them. I was suddenly afraid to look too closely at the windows. I could imagine what kinds of things might be out there. My glass of milk was still on the table and I went to pour it out in the sink. It had curdled to a thick, sour-smelling mess. I washed it down the drain, but I couldn't get the smell out of my nose as I crept back up to my room.

Macie was still asleep. It was hard to believe that just a few minutes ago I'd felt safe, like we could at least rest here for a while until we had to go back and figure out what to do next. That seemed like a million years ago.

Sleep was out of the question, and I didn't even want to take any more pictures of Macie in my bed, which should give a pretty good indication of how deeply distressed I was. I sat down by the foot of the bed and decided to stay on guard until the morning. This is easier in the movies, when you can just dissolve to the next scene without the long hours of actually sitting there. I couldn't do any of the normal things I did when I got freaked out in the middle of the night, namely turn on all the lights in the house and watch terrible late-night TV, so I just sat on the floor and stared. For a while, I watched the curtains, and soon I was convinced there was something behind them, clinging to the window ledge by its claws, waiting for its chance to strike. When that fear passed, I expected my door to squeak open at any moment and reveal something horrible. Or, even worse, my parents.

I kept this up for the next couple of hours, until the darkness outside started to turn blue with the coming dawn. I knew that I still had to come up with a plan to keep Macie hidden until my parents got out of the house, but the dawn had a strange effect on me. It was like I had finished a marathon and now couldn't take another step for love or money. I sighed and shook myself in an effort to stay awake, but all that did was remind me how stiff and sore I was. I'd be able to think a lot better if I just stretched out on the carpet for a minute. And that did it.

When I opened my eyes again, the clock by my bed said ten-thirty. Could that be right? Oh, God, where was everybody? I pulled myself up and took a few wobbly steps. Where was Macie? I looked around. I'd had a pair of old jeans hung on my chair, and now they were gone, along with the keys that had been on my dresser. Through the window, I saw that my car wasn't where I'd parked it. My bed had been loosely made up. I pulled back the sheets and picked up the pillow. It smelled like Macie's perfume. So last night had been real, after all. I took another deep breath of Macie's scent. I could have stayed in that moment forever and been perfectly happy to do so. But I couldn't. I put it down, probably with even more regret than when I was six years old and had to leave my stuffed frog at home to go to kindergarten.

I staggered into the bathroom with a growing recollection of everything that had happened last night. The first thing I did was throw up. When I was done, I felt better. Lighter, anyway. I washed my face in the sink, then brushed my teeth and went downstairs.

The house was empty. A glance out the window confirmed that Macie had indeed run off with my car. She must have made it out without running into my parents, because I certainly couldn't imagine being allowed to sleep through *that* discussion.

The question was, where did she go? Even if I knew that, how would I get there? All the cars were gone and ever since I'd gotten my license I'd had about as much use for my bike as for my old retainer. I was pretty sure the bike was out in the barn, but I had no idea where to find the air pump that I imagined the tires needed. Besides, it would take me half a day to ride into town, and then I would most likely get hit by a car at the first intersection.

Who did I know that could give me a ride? As I racked my brain, my eye fell on the kitchen calendar and I realized that I was scheduled to work today. In approximately nine minutes, in fact. I picked up the phone.

"Hello, Jaya's Authentic Foods. May I help you?"

"Hi, Nate. It's Hal. I've got a problem with my car. Is there any chance I could get a ride?"

"I'm in the middle of prep here."

"I know. I'm really sorry, but I don't know anybody else to call."

"Jaya's gonna be pissed."

"I know."

There was a pause while Nate weighed the options. Eventually, I heard a small sigh. "I'll be right there," he said.

"Thanks a lot. I really appreciate it."

I honestly did. The round trip from the restaurant to my house and back was about forty-five minutes, and neither of us could tell for sure how Jaya would react to getting stuck with the rest of the lunch prep and even a good chunk of the cooking.

And on top of that, I wasn't even going to show up at all.

As I waited for Nate I spent the time nervously watching the windows to make sure my mom didn't get back from wherever she was, notice my missing car, and start asking questions. I had a hard time sitting still. I ran my fingers over the kitchen counter where John Graze's runes had appeared. I couldn't decide if I was able to feel anything there—some residual scorches the eye couldn't see—or if I was imagining things. It didn't matter, really. The magic had done its job already. Nothing in the house felt like it should have. Everything seemed off in some way, like someone had gone through and subtly rearranged everything. I grabbed my spare keys from the hook by the back door, then went upstairs to get my camera. I told myself that I might need to take pictures of whatever was going to happen next, but more than that I think I wanted something familiar to hang on to, and it was either going to be the camera or the stuffed frog.

15

When Nate got there, I was out of the house and standing in the driveway before his Mini Cooper had even finished its turn. Nate was one of those huge guys who seem drawn to tiny cars, and as I climbed into the passenger side I got the brief impression that someone had stuffed a Kodiak bear behind the wheel.

"Thanks again," I said.

"Not a problem. So what happened to your car?"

"My girlfriend took it," I said. Why not be honest?

"How old are you?"

"Sixteen."

Nate grunted. "Starting early." He turned up the "unsigned alternative" station on his satellite radio and we drove on. We drove past the fields and the far-flung suburbs that separated my house from the beginnings of the city itself. We passed the giant corn chip processing plant and drove through Darmstadt, one of a dozen little towns around Lamasco, all founded by German immigrants a hundred and fifty years ago.

As we went through, Nate said, "This was where that kid lived, wasn't it?"

"Which kid?"

"Didn't you see the news this morning? Some kid took a double-bit axe and tried to smash in the door of a neighbor's house."

My mouth felt dry. "What was his name?"

"It was a girl. Alecia something. The cops had to shoot her with a stun gun."

"Alecia Nunn?" I don't know why I phrased it as a question. I knew already. She had been the in chorus in the play, one of William's friends.

"That's like the third or fourth kid this week," Nate said. "I guess somebody must be passing around some bad acid."

"Is that still a thing?"

"Looks like it to me."

Outside the windows, the houses were closer together now. I always thought it was neat that the road we were on went from the middle of the country to the middle of the city without ever turning. I took this route all the time when I was going to and from Jaya's, and it made me happy each time I drove it. There was no real reason why—just a bunch of things that I had seen ever since I was a kid, sitting in the back seat while Mom drove me to piano lessons or the orthodontist: Central

261

High School, Droste's jewelry shop, Wesselman's supermarket, the Donut Bank, and on and on.

I tried to pay attention to the landmarks to keep my mind off of other things. I was worried about where Macie had gone, and I was worried about what John Graze was going to do next. On top of that, I was still worried about what Micah had told me. I couldn't help myself. I didn't know if Micah, prompted by his sorcerous puppet master, was just poking at a weak spot of mine, or if he was actually right about Macie. Was she going to leave me? Was she going to leave me for Micah? It was easy to tell myself that it wasn't true, but I couldn't quite make myself believe it. I could make myself *want* to believe it, but that wasn't exactly the same thing.

We were getting toward the center of town. We had passed Deaconess Hospital and St. Anthony's Church, and I could see Willard Library getting closer on the left.

Suddenly I had a feeling about where to find Macie.

"Get on the Lloyd here," I said to Nate, pointing to the lane that led to the Lloyd Expressway on-ramp.

"Why?"

"Please. It's important."

Nate, bless him, shrugged his big shoulders and drifted into the other lane. He gunned the Mini's engine and merged onto the expressway. "You're not going to Jaya's?"

"Not today."

He sighed. "She's gonna have my ass for this. Yours, too."

"I know. I'm really sorry."

Nate nodded. "Tell me where to turn."

We got off on Vann Avenue and headed south toward the Book Broker. When we stopped, I could tell that Nate wasn't impressed. If I was going to ditch work, I could hear him think, couldn't I come up with something better to do than read comic books and look for old paperbacks?

"I wish I could explain this," I began.

"Is it about your girlfriend?"

"Yeah. Sort of."

"Well, I hope it works out." He dug a gas station receipt out of the center console and wrote something on the back. He handed it to me. "This is my cell number. Call me if you need anything, all right?"

"Thanks." I couldn't think of anything else to say. This sudden and unexpected evidence of Nate's humanity had left me speechless.

"Okay. I gotta go," Nate said. "I'll tell Jaya—I don't know. I'll tell her something, I guess. Don't take any bad acid."

"I'll do my best. Thanks again, Nate."

I watched him pull back into traffic, then I turned toward the Book Broker. I had the oddest feeling, and it took me a second to realize what it was. It was the same feeling I got at the beginning of a play, as I waited in the wings for my first entrance. Nervous. Anxious, but disassociated. Like it was someone else who was about to go out there, and it was his responsibility to get all the lines and moves right.

Inside the Book Broker, the haunted-looking clerk nodded at me as I passed by him and entered the used book section. The door to Calvin's office was just slightly open, like someone had tried to pull it closed but hadn't used enough force. With luck, Macie would still be inside, working on a way to get Calvin out of his little wooden prison so she could take revenge on John Graze.

Inside the office, there was no Macie, which was a disappointment, but it was clear that something had happened in here. All the loose paper had been organized and stacked in tidy piles, but that wasn't what grabbed my attention. On the desk, there was something that made me forget about everything else.

Calvin's box was closed, and as I watched, the sides and the top bowed outward then warped inward, as if it were a living thing laboring to breathe. I put aside my initial impulse, which was to swat it into the wastebasket, and got closer. The sheer unnaturalness of it made my skin crawl, the way it might if your pencil ever grew legs like a millipede and began to crawl around your desk.

"Calvin?" I called. No response. I reached out and picked up the box. I could feel the wood straining.

"Calvin, I'm going to open the box." When I didn't hear a tiny "No, wait!" from inside, I put my thumbs on the corners of the lid and pushed upward.

As soon as I applied pressure, the box just exploded. That's the best way I can describe it. Bits of it went everywhere and for an instant I had visions of being mutilated by slivers of wood traveling at supersonic speed, but most of it was nothing more than sawdust. Of course, I only realized this after I had thrown myself onto the couch and buried my head in the cushions for a few seconds.

On the desk was a semi-transparent, egg-shaped glob of jelly, about as large as my fist. Inside was a toy-sized figure of a man. As I watched, the gray glob quivered and the figure inside got bigger. As it grew, the jelly stretched and expanded. Soon, the figure was half as big as I was, and the gray stuff was stretched thinly over him like a film. There was a snapping sound, like someone had stretched a large rubber band too far, and the film broke apart in a cloud of gray vapor.

Calvin sat on the desk, normal-sized once more.

We stared at each other for a few seconds without saying anything. My eyes were watering and my throat was sore from the gray vapor. Calvin hopped to the floor. He wobbled a little, but steadied himself with a hand on the desk. He didn't look any different. His beard hadn't gone gray and his round cheeks hadn't turned hollow. He was wearing blue plaid flannel pajama pants and a dingy white t-shirt that said "Ohio Renaissance Festival 1992" on it. He still hadn't said a word, and I had the awful idea that he might have lost his mind. He looked at me thoughtfully, then scampered across the office and flung open the door. This utterly terrified a girl with black hair and a motorcycle jacket, who had been browsing in the used romance novels.

"Sorry," Calvin mumbled as she knelt down to pick up the stack of paperbacks she'd flung into the air. He eased the door closed and leaned against it.

"Hi," I said.

"I guess I'm free," he said.

"It looks that way."

"I'm really free." He opened the office door again, heard the startled shriek it produced, then closed it. He ran his fingers over the starburst of singed wood chips that had been his prison. "It's been... It's been a very long time. And it hasn't. I'm not sure exactly. Everything feels like it's moving very quickly, and like it's standing still." He blinked and took a couple of deep breaths. "How are you?"

I didn't doubt that Calvin's captivity had put him under some stress, but I didn't have time to wait until he was fully recovered.

"Calvin, have you seen Macie today?" I asked.

"Today? How long has it been today?"

Oh, crap. That wasn't going to work. "Do you remember the last time you talked to Macie? What did she talk to you about?"

"Yeah. It was weird. That was today?"

"What was it, Calvin?"

"She said she was ready to help get me out. She even smashed the spell on the door, just to show she was ready to do real magic. But she had a lot of questions about some of the other things she'd read. Some of it was really technical. I was surprised she'd understood so much of it. You know, I don't think I've ever seen anyone take to magic the way she has. She's picked it up so fast."

"That's what I'm afraid of. What kind of things did she ask about?"

"Like how we were going to stop John Graze's rituals. What my plans were, based on what I knew about him. She wouldn't stop asking. I got the impression she wanted to know all this before she would let me out."

Calvin pushed himself away from the door and took a step, then clutched at his stomach and nearly doubled over. He looked up at me. "All of a sudden, I am really, really hungry. Can we go get something to eat?"

Outside the office, Calvin walked slowly, running his fingers over everything and breathing deeply the smell of old paperbacks and sweat. He acted like someone who hadn't seen any of this for a long, long time. When I told him I didn't have a car, he drifted over to the front counter, where the clerk had been watching our approach with undisguised fear.

Calvin nodded at him. "Toby."

"Hi, Calvin," he said meekly.

"We need your car."

Without another word, the counter guy fished around in his pocket and came up with a couple of keys on a Wonder Woman keychain. He held it out to Calvin with two fingers.

"What was that about?" I asked when we were out in the parking lot and scanning around for Toby's Chevy Citation.

"I hate to admit it, but the fact is, Toby always thought I was kind of a dangerous eccentric."

I had little trouble imagining that, but I kept this observation to myself. We found Toby's car. "Do you mind driving?" he asked as he patted the pockets of his pajama pants. "I always feel nervous driving without my license."

Our first stop was a Walgreens on Washington Avenue, where I bought Calvin a pair of flip-flops, which instantly upgraded his appearance from "escaped mental patient" to "mental patient out on temporary furlough." It wasn't much, but it was enough to keep us from getting kicked out of Sir Beef.

We picked up our order at the counter and sat in one of the Olde English-style wooden booths, under a window treated to look like stained glass. Calvin had ordered six roast beef sandwiches, along with fries and a jumbo Coke, all of which I paid for. I let him eat the first couple in peace, but once he started to slow down I pressed him for more details about what had happened today.

"She was determined," Calvin began as I dipped a couple of my fries into the container of horseradish sauce. I wasn't hungry, but I thought I should eat something to keep him company. Besides, I'd thrown up everything I'd eaten the day before, so I probably needed a bite. "Once she disintegrated the locking spell on the door, she said she was ready to get me out. I remember she said she wasn't going to wait anymore." Calvin chewed thoughtfully for a second. "Once I was sure she knew what to do, she started the spell."

Real magic, I thought. Macie was doing real magic. "Did it work?" I asked.

"Well, here I am. Apparently, it did. But not right away."

"What went wrong?"

"Wrong? Nothing. As I said before, she is tremendously talented at this. But that spell, once it's been said, takes effect over a period of hours. There are others that do the same thing a whole lot faster, but I'd been teaching her the slow one. That way, as I returned to the real world, I'd be able to see how I was progressing, and hopefully make adjustments if I had to. The others? With those, I'm there, and then—boom!—I'm here. Or possibly somewhere else entirely. No margin for error."

"That makes sense."

"You'd think so. But when Macie realized it was going to be hours before I returned all the way, she got upset."

"What did she do then?"

"I'm not sure. The gray film was already closing around me, and that made it hard to see much of anything. Then she moved out of my line of vision. I saw her a few times after that, but I couldn't say anything to her. She leaned over the box once and I could see her lips move, but that was all. After that she closed the lid and I was too busy making sure I was headed in the right direction to notice anything else. The next person I saw was you."

"I think she went to find John Graze."

Instead of choking on his soda, Calvin just nodded. "She wouldn't be the first person to try something like that."

"She probably took whatever she could find in your notes that she thought would help her, then went to go get him."

"Is this because of her sister?"

"I think so." I gave him a summary of last night's events, including Sandra's full-on freakout and the visitation by John Graze, while he ate another sandwich.

"Thanks for not killing me," Calvin said when I was finished.

"I would have said whatever he wanted," I admitted. "I was terrified."

"You had good reason to be. This is bad, Hal. It may be even worse now. I understand why Macie did what she did, but I wish she would have waited for me."

"I think she had it in her mind that the longer she waited, the worse things were going to get," I said. "She couldn't sit still any longer."

"I said she was talented, and she really is, but that's not everything. Even if you were born to be the best baseball player in the world, there's not much chance you'll hit a home run if you go up against Hank Aaron with only a couple days' worth of practice."

"I don't think Hank Aaron was a pitcher."

"Same difference. We have to go after Graze now. As much as I'd like to have my notes, some other sorcerers, or even something besides pajamas to wear, we've got to do it now. Maybe we can find Macie before she tries anything."

"Sounds good," I said.

Honestly, this didn't sound good at all, but he was right. We had to do it. We were all that was left. Besides, I was ditching work anyway. I might as well make the day count. "What do we do first?"

"That's a good question." Calvin searched around in the ice at the bottom of his cup for any remaining soda, making a snorkeling sound with his straw. "His creatures feed on emotional upheaval. That's where they get their power. We should keep ourselves from getting emotional."

"Screw that. Emotional is all I know how to be."

Calvin laughed, which was the first time I'd ever seen him do that. "True, true." He stopped to sigh and pat his stomach gingerly. Four sandwiches seemed to have taken a toll. He stood up and swept the wrappers and debris onto his tray. He handed me the two leftover sandwiches, still wrapped up in their crimson Sir Beef foil paper. "We may need those in the future."

"So if the creatures are all connected to John Graze," I said, thinking out loud, "then he gets stronger as they get stronger."

"They also connect the victims to him. The victims become a part of him, just like the creatures are a part of him."

"It's what he used to have as a rock star," I realized. "Thousands of people who can't take their eyes off of him. That's what he wants again."

"If we damage those connections, maybe we can ruin his performance, so to speak," Calvin said. "Break his spell."

"And then what?" I asked as we left. Outside of the air-conditioned restaurant, the heat hit us like a sledgehammer.

"And then I don't know. The magic could just fade away and leave him free to try again. It could rebound on him in some destructive way. It could rebound on *all* of us in some destructive way. I've got no way to know for sure."

We climbed into the car and I started it up.

"But it's the only idea we have," Calvin said. "If Macie's gotten in over her head, this may be the only way to help her."

I turned onto Lincoln Avenue and headed back across town.

"Where are you going?" Calvin asked.

"His house is just ashes now. If he's anywhere, it has to be at the Alhambra."

Calvin nodded and leaned back in his seat. He put his fingertips together and closed his eyes. He was either meditating to gather his sorcerous power, or trying to digest four roast beef sandwiches. Either way, I didn't want to disturb him.

I drove past my eye doctor's office, then the upscale funeral home where my grandmother's funeral had been, and after that the University of Lamasco campus. I tried not to think that I might be seeing them all for the last time. We crossed Highway 41, which divided the town in half. This was where the older neighborhoods started. The houses here were huge: tall multi-story things with columned porches and cupolas. Most of them were falling apart, with broken windows and junk piled up by the doors, but a few showed some signs of life. With those, the grass was cut and there were colorful little beds of flowers along the sidewalk. Whenever I came down here, which was not often, since nobody in this neighborhood seemed to want any Korean food, I always wondered which way the neighborhood was heading: toward the flower beds or toward the broken windows.

After turning down a few side streets, we were on Governor Street, just a few blocks from the Alhambra.

"What do you want me to do?" I asked as we sat at a stoplight. Through the treetops, I could see the tip of one of the Alhambra's minarets.

"We should park," Calvin said.

"Out in the open?"

"It's not like he won't know we're here."

I parked in the community center's parking lot, separated from the Alhambra by a little concrete plaza. As soon as we got out I spotted a familiar car in front of an apartment building across the street. It was my car, which meant we were right about where Macie had gone, barring the unlikely event that she had felt like browsing at some art galleries this morning. The car's doors were locked, with the keys presumably in Macie's pocket. Or, really, my pocket, in my jeans, held up around Macie's hips by my belt. In other circumstances, that would have been a pretty sexy thought.

I still had my spare keys with me, and for a split second, I thought about jumping in the car and just driving away. But the idea passed.

Calvin put his hand on my shoulder. "It's time to go."

When we turned to face the Alhambra, both of us felt an invisible sort of power in the air. It was a thudding pulse of energy, like a massive electrical transformer, something we heard with our bones instead of our ears.

"This is definitely the right place," Calvin said.

The streets were completely bare. No hipsters. No poor kids. No social workers. No artists. Not even a stray plastic bag in the wind. Nothing moved at all.

"He's turned up the power," Calvin said. "Things are coming to a head."

"The big finish," I said.

We crossed the street and cut through the weedy square of ground behind the theater. We stopped at the steel door under the fire escape at the back of the building.

I put my hand on the wall. I could feel it hum.

"All right," Calvin said. "I don't know what's going to happen inside here, but I'm confident I can stop him. We don't know where Macie is, so there's a chance you may have to help her while I deal with John. Stay as close to me as you can, though. I'll be able to provide some protection from whatever he can conjure up, but don't take any risks if you don't have to."

Calvin twisted the handle and pushed the door open. We stood there for a second, looking into the blackness within.

"Well—" Calvin began. An instant later, he froze. I saw him stiffen, then wobble slightly. At the same time, he started to change color. Not just the bits of his face visible above the beard, but all of him—hair, clothes, skin—everything darkened and turned a deep jade green as cracks appeared all over and raced up and down his body. Then, with a sound like someone smashing a watermelon, Calvin fell apart.

As the pieces hit the ground, each one became a fat, dark-green bullfrog. Before I could even move, all that was left of Calvin was a couple dozen frogs, all hopping in different directions, trying to escape.

16

I staggered backward and managed not to step on any of the frogs, which was lucky. If I had, I probably would have lost my mind.

I could barely breathe. Calvin was gone. He had been turned into a rain of frogs, all rapidly disappearing under bushes and into storm drains. John Graze had gotten him. John Graze had probably gotten Macie, too. Now I was the only one left.

What could I do? Nothing. There was nothing I could do. My mind was a flickering jumble of frogs and monsters.

I took another step backward. My car was just across the street. I could get in the car, drive to Jaya's, apologize for being late, and pretend all this had never happened. Would that work?

Probably not.

But something else might.

I ran toward my car, but I wasn't running away. I had an idea.

I threw open the car door and knelt on the front seat. There, in the cup holder where I had left it, was Calvin's charm. That folded-up scrap of paper, tied with yellow string, that I had grabbed off of Macie's dresser last night.

I put it around my neck. Calvin had once said it would help keep me safe. It had helped me see things inside of John Graze's house, and I was pretty sure it had helped Macie see what had happened to her sister, too. Would it be enough to protect me from whatever was behind the Alhambra door?

I didn't know, but I was about to find out. I stood up straight and took a deep breath. Macie hadn't run away from John Graze. Calvin hadn't run away. And as much as I wanted to, I wasn't going to run away, either.

Before I had a chance to lose my nerve, I marched back to the theater door. I reached for the handle, turned it, and jumped to the side.

No blast of magic force. No frogs. Nothing. Yet.

I could see the short hall that led to the darkened backstage area. I stepped inside and closed the door behind me, then gripped the charm around my neck. I half-expected the packet of paper to feel warm, but it felt just the way it always did, like folded-up notebook paper wrapped in thread and hanging around the neck of a terrified guy.

Once the door was closed, I could see a weak glow of light spilling around the obstacles ahead of me. I crept forward and saw that the stage lights were on, and streaks of light poked through the threadbare backdrop curtain.

The hum of power was very loud now. It came from all directions, and there was something else, too. A sort of wet clicking, chittering sound that made me think of slime-coated eels with long, sharp teeth. As I moved through the backstage area I could see things, too. Nothing obvious, just odd shadows and motion where nothing should be moving, the kind of thing you think you see from the corner of your eye when you're tired or stressed. I was tired *and* stressed, of course, but these things were happening right in front of me and I knew I wasn't imagining them.

I reached one of the wings and leaned around to get a look at what was happening on stage. There was John Graze, in the center of a huge pattern drawn on the black-painted boards with yellow chalk. The chalk had been overlaid with ropes of electric lights, tiny blue ones that were nothing more than pinpoints under the hot white glare of the spotlight. At first, the lights and the chalk drawings were just a jumble of curves and lines, but an instant later I recognized them. They formed a pentagram within a pentagram, the symbol that had been on Left Hand Ritual's first album and had served as an unofficial logo ever since, right up until John quit and the rest of the band tried to go in a more pop direction.

He looked rougher than he had last night, in the vision—or apparition, or whatever you call it—in my kitchen. He was sweating, like he had spent long hours in this un-air-conditioned building, and his black clothes were streaked with chalk and grime.

He was chanting softly. I couldn't hear him, but I could see his lips move as he stared into the empty theater. Every time he stopped at the end of a phrase, I felt another throb of power radiate outward from the center of the pentagrams. He had hung a black banner above the left side of the stage. The ten-foot-tall banner showed a figure sitting cross-legged with its hands raised, palms out. The body had no clothes, and was half male and half female, but the head was that of a long-horned bull with human-shaped eyes. Behind the figure and all over its body were symbols and formulas, all done in silver thread that gleamed in the spotlight. I recognized some of them from Calvin's papers and some of them from the paintings on the walls of John Graze's nest.

Under that banner was a thick fake-stone pedestal with a brass bowl on it. There was one on my side of the stage, too, and I assumed there was a banner hanging above it as well, at an angle I couldn't see. This all tugged at something in the back of my mind. It was more than just creepy set dressing. It meant something. Then I remembered: This was the stage set that Left Hand Ritual had used on the *Controller of the Real* tour, the one where the band had fallen apart halfway through. I had seen pictures on fan sites and in the liner notes of the crappy live album that Titan records had put out to complete the band's contract.

I tried to remember what the entire set had looked like. On that tour they'd mounted a gigantic metal-frame star so that it towered above the drum riser, then they'd strapped a dancer onto the crossbeam, and she'd play the "sacrificial victim" role at the climax of the song "Overlord." This was what really got them in the gunsights of the Parents' Music Resource Council, and the people who still remember Left Hand Ritual tend to remember them as "that band that killed women on stage."

I edged out of the wings a little and shifted around so I could see more of the stage. There was no star this time, and no drum riser, either. Just a tall metal arch and above it, ten feet in the air, was Macie.

She was hovering there, with no supports or wires or anything, just suspended in the air, in defiance of gravity. I suppose that with everything else I'd seen, it shouldn't have been that big of a deal, but the absolute unnaturalness of it still made me want to look away. Macie's eyes were open. They weren't focused, and I don't think she was actually seeing anything.

The pulses of energy, which had been as regular as a heartbeat, now stopped.

"You should come out now, Hal," John Graze said from inside his pentagram. His voice sounded rough, but it still had a lot of the eerie power that I remembered from last night.

His creatures must have been watching me ever since I came in, so I assumed my choice was either to step out or be dragged out. I took a deep breath and walked out on the stage.

"Hi," I said. I know, I know. But what are you supposed to say in situations like this?

"Are you going to try, too?" he asked. "Do you have some other scraps of magic from that fat idiot that you'd like to throw at me? I should have set traps for both of you, not just him."

"Hal?" Macie called. She sounded confused and distant, like someone with a high fever.

Beneath her, the space inside the metal arch was subtly different from the space around it. Darker. More purple. Like the skin of an eggplant.

I could see the dim shapes of his creatures now, like misty ghosts walking around us. One of them was behind me. It reached out and I jumped forward.

John Graze laughed. John Graze laughing sounded even more frightening then John Graze being threatening.

"Well, it looks like you've got some sort of magic after all. Did Calvin give you a charm? Can you see things you're not supposed to see? Maybe you've picked up a couple of magic words like this one?" He nodded toward Macie.

"You should take a seat and watch, then. You might as well learn something while you're here." He pointed to the row of decaying seats in front of the stage. There were creatures almost all around me now. The only way to move was in the direction he was pointing. I let myself down from the stage before I could be pushed.

"Hal!" Macie was looking at me now. She seemed to be waking up.

"I'm sorry," I said. The shadowy creatures herded me to a front-row center seat. I wanted to say something else to Macie, something like "it's going to be all right," but I didn't have a whole lot of confidence about that.

"You," John Graze said to me, "you're useless. But she has all sorts of potential. I could feel that the first time I met her. It's that potential that will make her the perfect sacrifice, and keep the gate open forever."

He knelt down and picked up a huge knife, the same one we'd seen him use in his back yard.

"If you don't give up something valuable, it's not a sacrifice," he said. "It's a shame, though. She would have been wonderful. Once my creatures were through with her."

Macie shouted insults down at John, who just shrugged.

He turned back to me. "Once you're one of us, there might be something I can do with you," he said. "Maybe not. For now, though, you need to watch me.

You need to see what no one has ever seen, or ever will again."

The knot of creatures drifted away from me, though I knew there were still hundreds nearby, and more on the other side of that purple-lit gate. John Graze began to chant again. At first his voice sounded just as it had when he was talking to me, but then it started to get softer, as if he were walking away. As his voice faded, the throbbing pulses of energy returned and soon I couldn't hear his words anymore. Instead, I could *feel* them.

His chant continued and I noticed that he kept looking down at me. At first I thought he wanted to make sure I wasn't going to run, but then I realized the truth: He was performing. He wanted to see how I was reacting to the show. Whatever else his creatures did for him, they didn't give him the satisfaction of performing in front of an audience, even if that audience was just me.

Then the significance of the stage dressing hit me. The lights, the bull-man banners, the columns, the sacrificial victim floating above, it was all set up to match the last moments of his time with his band. He was going to rewrite that part of his history. Instead of it being the moment where his power as a musician collapsed, it was now going to be the moment where his power as a warlock became complete. In a way, it was fascinating, like getting a peek into someone else's mind. Someone else's horrible, insane mind.

I leaned forward. There didn't seem to be any kind of magical power holding me to my seat, and all the creatures in the theater were paying much more attention to John Graze than to me.

Maybe I could do something. I leaned over to look in the orchestra pit. There wasn't much there, just a couple of bent music stands, some folding chairs, and some two-by-fours and boxes of nails left over from a previous attempt at rehabilitating the building. It was enough to get me thinking, though.

I waited until the next throb of energy had passed over me. Then, before another one could build, I leaned back, cupped my hands to my mouth and yelled.

"Boo!"

This was a lot louder than I had expected it to be. Despite the waves of magical energy and all the shadowy creatures hovering around, the place was nearly silent. That was fine, though. I wasn't going to stop now.

"You suck! Boo! Get off the stage!"

John stared down at me. His face was a mix of disbelief and hatred.

"Boring! Boring! We saw this in 1985! You suck! Get off the stage! Boo!"

Behind him, Macie had begun to twirl and drift slowly in the air, like a decorative mobile hung up in a draft.

John's face was twisted with anger. "You! Shut it!" he called.

I switched on my camera flash and took a couple of pictures, just to be extra-irritating. "*Second Sunrise* was the only good album Left Hand Ritual ever did!" I yelled. That was hitting below the belt. *Second Sunrise* was the band's last album, made long after John had left, and many of the songs were widely believed to be thinly-veiled swipes at him by the rest of the band.

As painful as it had been for me to say that (*Second Sunrise* was a really terrible album), it did what I wanted. John looked like he was ready to jump out of his pentagram and beat me senseless, and Macie spun and twisted erratically as his concentration waned. She was getting closer to the floor every second.

John gestured to where a knot of his creatures were lurking. "Get him! Destroy him!"

"God, you're a prima donna!" I shouted as I stood up. "The rest of the band was right." I leaned over the broken railing of the orchestra pit and pulled something up. "If you can't take a little criticism, get off the damn stage!" Then I threw a folding chair at him.

That must have done it. To have this pivotal moment, this rewriting of his history, end up just as it did the first time, with a chair sailing toward his head, must have pushed him over the edge. That inaudible sensation of magical energy drained away like someone had kicked out a power cord. Macie dropped the last two feet to the stage and collapsed in front of the metal arch. The spotlight shining on the silver threads in the banners grew dimmer, and even John Graze seemed like less of a god-like rock star and more like a sweaty middle-aged guy who hadn't washed for a couple of days.

"You fucking *worm!*" he snarled, then began to chant again. This time I could hear it all: flat, rapid syllables that I couldn't understand but recognized as something incredibly venomous and hateful.

His creatures must have understood it perfectly, though. They perked right up as soon as the new chant began. They spread out like wolves and closed in around me. I could see more of them on stage, too, pouring out from the wings and drawing in toward Macie, who had just stumbled to her feet.

"Macie!" I shouted. I ripped Calvin's charm from around my neck and tossed it to her. I throw about as well as any other member of the drama club, so the folded paper hit the stage a good fifteen feet in front of her. It skidded a few feet farther, and Macie rushed forward to pick it up from there.

Now that I had gotten rid of the charm, I could no longer see any of the shadow creatures. Even the stage decorations were hazy. But I could see Macie, tearing through the thread that held the charm together, and I could see John Graze, continuing to chant and sneering at me with a triumphant look in his eyes.

I couldn't see the creatures, but I could feel them. Cold, rubbery, invisible hands grabbed me. And they didn't just grab onto me, they grabbed *through* me. Those fingers and claws pushed through my skin and into my bones, turning them to ice. I felt them push into my skull and my mind became covered with frozen fog and my eyes were blinded with purplish flickering static. The last thing I heard was Macie's voice, louder than I had ever heard it before, shouting more words that I couldn't understand.

17

And that was pretty much the end of anyone's hope for a Left Hand Ritual reunion. I didn't remember anything that happened after I threw the charm to Macie, but she described it to me later. Once she had the charm, she could tell from the bits of writing visible on the outside that there was some sort of magical formula folded up in there. Fortunately, she had learned enough about magic (and Calvin's handwriting) to be able to read it the way it had to be read.

After she tore open the paper and shouted out the syllables, she could, in her words, "see everything." That meant not only the creatures, but also the lines of magical power that connected them, the gate, the pentagram, and John Graze himself. She even saw what John looked like "underneath his face," as she put it. She would never tell me what that looked like, and I haven't pressed her about it.

With that vision came some kind of power, too. The creatures couldn't touch her, and they acted like they didn't even want to try. Macie wasn't sure what to do next, but she figured the best choice would be to destroy something. She picked up the folding chair I'd thrown and slammed it into the side of the metal arch.

The arch pitched over and clattered to the ground. John bellowed with anger and spun around, but it was too late. Macie had grabbed the tangle of wires and lights that formed his pentagram and pulled as hard as she could. There was a huge hissing sound, like air rushing out of a giant balloon, and the lines of magical power that connected everything faded and flickered out. The creatures, even the ones that were busy attacking me, looked up and turned their blank faces to John. He frantically tried to shove Macie away, but recoiled as if she were too hot to touch. He scrambled to reshape his pentagram from the tangle of cables, but he ran out of time. The creatures were all around him.

As they reached him, they seemed to dive inside of him, creature after creature disappearing into him. With each one, he seemed to get darker and more purplish until, when the last of the creatures was gone, what stood there was a hybrid thing, glistening and purple, with a round mouth full of shark's teeth, but with bulging, human eyes that glared at Macie with a mixture of rage and fear. It stood there for a second, then dissolved into a haze of eggplant-colored smoke that vanished in the glare of the spotlight.

Instead of fainting dead away, which is what I would have done, Macie leaped off the stage and slapped me back to consciousness. She helped me walk, still shivering, out of the Alhambra and back to my car. She drove until we got to Willard Library, which felt like a safe distance, then we sat on a park bench and she explained what had happened since I passed out.

"I think he's gone," Macie said at the end. "I can't explain how, but I just didn't *feel* him anymore."

"That sounds good enough for me." I stood up and stretched. I still felt a little feverish, like I could have used a jacket even though it was over ninety degrees outside. But the sick feeling was fading fast.

When we got back to Macie's house, her parents' car was in the driveway, as was an ambulance. Her parents, upon returning from their trip, had found Sandra sprawled unconscious in the foyer and broken glass all over the living room. Sandra, they said, had taken a bad fall on the stairs and somehow managed to smash the front window in the process. A quick trip to the hospital showed no damage beyond a few cuts and bruises, and as time went by, the lingering symptoms of Sandra's first "concussion" vanished completely. No one could say why, and while their doctor didn't agree that the second injury had knocked right what the first one had knocked loose, he did say that the brain did a lot of things that no one understood yet. That was hardly the kind of thing you want to hear from a physician, and Macie and I certainly had a better explanation, but we kept it to ourselves. We were just happy to see evidence of John Graze's magic fading away.

It wasn't just Sandra, either. There were no more reports of kids from the musical cast going berserk, and William and the girls who had run away quickly returned to sanity. Eventually, people settled on the explanation that someone had spiked the drinks at the cast party with some sort of wildly potent and dangerous drugs. There was a short investigation as to who might have been responsible, but nothing ever came of it. I heard through Macie, who heard through a friend, that Micah never figured out where his massive collection of bruises had come from, and became the poster boy for the unfortunate victims of the mad drink-spiker.

But that was all in the future. The day after we escaped from John Graze, we went back to the Alhambra. The neighborhood didn't look so deserted this time, and I got a pang when I saw the car Calvin and I had borrowed from Toby sitting there, abandoned. The back door of the theater was still unlocked. When we went in, neither of us could feel anything unusual. We saw nothing strange, and there were no "vibes" suggesting creatures watching us from the shadows. The banners and props had rotted, as if they'd been left in a damp storeroom for thirty years. The metal arch still lay on the stage. It was tarnished and corroded, and there was a big crack across its top.

"Was it like that before?" I asked.

"I have no idea. I was a little busy."

I touched the arch and it broke apart along the crack, the two halves rattling against the stage and making us jump.

"I can't help but think that's a good sign," I said.

We explored around a little more, but neither of us really felt there was anything to find. Whatever magic that had been here was gone. But the trip wasn't a total waste of time. I was nosing around in the box office, keeping low in order not to be seen from the street, when I found a full case of Polaroid SX-70 film under a pile of old newspapers. Now, for those of you who don't know, finding Polaroid film is like finding gold, and I carried it off to the car with a big stupid grin on my face. The film was expired, but that was just as good, since it gave the pictures a hazy, washed-out look that's really nice if you like that kind of thing. Later on, Macie even posed for a couple of shots to test it out for me, including a very nice one where she's looking back over her bare shoulder. Not exactly a figure study, but it was a good start.

We drove Toby's car back to the Book Broker. I stepped inside, caught his eye, and slid the key across the counter to him. He was probably going to have questions, and any answers I could give weren't going to make him feel any better, so I just shrugged and ran.

I never heard anything else about John Graze, not even a newspaper report mentioning his burned-out house. I drove past it once, after making a late delivery for Jaya's, and it was indeed nothing but a charred shell. Whatever had happened to him must have undone his illusions. If anyone ever wondered where he went, they probably figured that the reclusive former heavy metal star had gone into even deeper seclusion after the destruction of his home. That's the explanation I would have given if anybody asked me about it, but of course no one ever did.

When I got back to my job, Jaya wasn't even mad that I had missed my shift (as well as the ones for the next day). Nate, to my surprise, had come up with a cover story that made me sound like a hero for even trying to come to work despite horrifying personal circumstances. I asked him what he had actually told her, but all I got was a baritone chuckle before he went back to the chicken he was cooking. I had planned to quit Jaya's once school started, but now I may see if I can swing things to keep working. I like it there.

The SMRC people, like the rest of John Graze's victims, seemed to recover from their demonic experience without a clear memory of what had happened. Macie and I started going to the SMRC meetings in the repaired basement of St. Mark's, mainly to see if anyone could explain what had happened to Calvin, but also to find someone who could help Macie make more sense of the notes she'd taken from his office. So far, none of them remember ever having heard of Calvin, and no one seems to know anything about magic anymore, despite the pretty heavy hints we keep dropping. Either their minds have been erased on that topic or they're still testing us. I'm starting to lean toward the former.

But it's still fun. A couple of the guys, Ragnar and Moonwulf, are my age, and they're teaching me to swordfight, while the sewing guild has helped Macie construct an astonishingly low-cut bodice that she plans to show off at the next demonstration day. It didn't take us long to feel pretty comfortable there. SMRC people aren't fundamentally too different from drama club people, though they are just a shade weirder. Drama club people at least know how to *pretend* to be normal most of the time. However, at the SMRC, we get to use real swords and axes. That pretty much evens things out, I think.

I missed Calvin a lot. He had been goofy and strange, and I never felt like I really knew him all that well, but I thought we could have been friends. I felt bad that we wouldn't have the chance.

Also, I kept on listening to Left Hand Ritual. I knew I probably shouldn't, but a favorite band is a favorite band. What can you do?

I was thinking about all this as I sat with Macie on the floor her room. I was resting on her hip, watching the end of a gladiator movie while Macie studied more of Calvin's notes. She tells me that this stuff makes much more sense than it used to. I have to take her word for it, since I've never been able to get anything out of them myself. She thinks she's about ready to try some of the formulas out for real.

I ran my hand down her thigh and stood up. I was a little worried still. Not about Macie trying the spells, though there were plenty of reasons for someone to be worried about that. I kept thinking about Macie and me. I couldn't get Micah's words completely out of my head. I hated the idea of anything coming between us, especially after all that had happened, but I still had that fear. Soon school would start, with new classes and a new play for us to be in, and I could remember the longing looks that Moonwulf and Ragnar had given her at the SMRC meetings. Would any of these end up drawing us apart? I hoped not.

I walked over to the window. On the driveway I saw three dark blobs lined up in a row. I reached for Macie's desk and picked up my latest garage-sale find, which I had been tinkering with earlier. It was a Canon 35mm camera from the Seventies with a half-stuck zoom lens on the front. I took a closer look at the blobs, which turned out to be what I thought they were: frogs. Three fat, dark-green frogs. I snapped a picture and put down the camera. Two days ago there had been only one. I wondered how many there would be tomorrow, and the day after that.

Macie was still lying on the rug, studying. I sat down beside her again and kissed her cheek.

She looked up at me.

"I'm happy to be here," I said.

"Me, too."

We kissed again, for a long time. We would see what happened.

www.ingramcontent.com/pod-product-compliance
Lightning Source LLC
Chambersburg PA
OBHW061341170010
46811CB00001B/62

*9 7 8 1 7 3 3 7 2 9 1 0 9 *